MOON RABBIT

By Oliver Eade

Illustrations by Alma Dowle

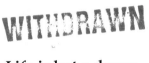

Life is but a dream
– Li Bo

*The school and the characters in this story, apart from
Mr Donald Gordon, Trimontium Trust, Melrose, are fictitious.*

dp Delancey Press
London 2009

Published by Delancey Press Ltd
23 Berkeley Square
London W1J 6HE

www.delanceypress.com

First published 2009
Cover illustration by Alma Dowle
Designed and typeset by Alan Simpson
Printed and bound in the UK by T. J. International Ltd

A CIP catalogue record for this title is available from the British Library

ISBN 978-1-907205-12-5

Acknowledgements

I am grateful to Liu Ping for his helpful advice; to Ken Teh for the calligraphy and to David Jones for his much-valued opinion and proofreading skills. I am indebted to Jenni Polson, Ellen Renton and Grace Inglis for their invaluable comments, as well as those other children and friends who kindly read the script. Finally I wish to thank my wife, Yvonne Wei-Lun, for her endless support and encouragement.

Dedicated to the memory of Dr Chen Yao-Sheng, a kind and loving Chinese Kung-Kung to my children, who taught me so much about his country's great civilisation, and who gave me the most wonderful thing of my life...the hand of his daughter, Wei-Lun, in marriage.

Oliver Eade

CONTENTS

Chapter 1   The Ducklings .... Page   1

Chapter 2   The Unhappy Dragon... Page 23

Chapter 3   The Qilin .... Page 49

Chapter 4   The Lady Silkworm.. Page 59

Chapter 5   Monkey King .... Page 69

Chapter 6   The Grey Tortoise and the Black Tortoise .... Page 89

Chapter 7   Moon Rabbit .... Page 107

Chapter 8   Changes at the Roman Camp .... Page 125

PRONUNCIATION OF PINYIN

The Chinese words in this story are Romanised as '**pinyin**'. **Pinyin** is a way of writing Chinese using our own Romanised phonetic script, but the pronunciation isn't always as might be expected when you see Chinese words written in **pinyin**:

- For example '*xi*' sounds like '**she**'. Thus '*xie xie*' (thank you) sounds like '**sheer sheer**' and '*xing*' (okay) sounds like '**shing**'.

- '*Qi*' sounds like '**chee**...' as in cheese. Therefore *Qilin*, the mythical Chinese beast made up from different animals, is pronounced '**chee-lin**'.

- In '*dui*', which means 'yes', the '*-ui*' is pronounced '**way**'. Thus '*dui*' becomes '**dway**'.

- In '*zai jian*' (good-bye) the '*-ai*' sounds like '*-ie*' in **pie**.

- '*Zh*' sounds like our '**J**', so '*zhong*' (clock) sounds like '**jong**' and '*Hangzhou*', the home city of our heroine, sounds like '**Hang-jow**'.

- The '*-ao*' in '*ni hao!*' (hallo) is pronounced '**ow**'. Therefore '*ni hao*' sounds a bit like '**knee how**'!

CHAPTER 1: THE DUCKLINGS

It was the first day back at Stevie Scott's school in Peebles, in the Scottish Borders, after the summer half-term break. Stevie felt really happy that day and there was a very good reason for this. As well as being a schoolboy Stevie was a Roman legionary together with his friend, Andy Watson. Stevie's *real* name was Stevius Maximus, and Andy, being shorter, was Andius Minimus. They had a Roman camp on the bank of the River Tweed just beyond the bridge. Their camp was an outpost of the better known Trimontium fort at Melrose, but it was a *secret* camp, which is why it was so important in the overall Roman military campaign. And, of course, being back at school meant that the legionaries would be able to discuss tactics together. Also, as the summer evenings were now long, they could spend more time at the camp. During the break Stevie had gone there in the early mornings too, and he was desperate to tell Andy about the duck family he had seen each day. There was a mother duck who lead her little troupe of five baby ducklings down to the water every morning to practise their swimming just in front of the camp.

At school that morning Stevie, who sat next to Andy, was going to tell his friend about the duck family when his attention was diverted. He was surprised to see a new girl in the class.

"I think she must be Chinese or Japanese, or something," he whispered to Andy.

"Are they at war with the Romans?" Andy whispered back.

Stevie didn't answer. He stared at the girl who had silky, black hair tied back into a ponytail with a pink hair-band, and Stevie thought she had prettiest face he had ever seen. She looked a little anxious, and Stevie realised she had good reason to feel like that since she'd been put next to Red-Nosed Rosie. Rosie hung around with Crazy Davie and Muckle Mikey and as well as being dim she was a real trouble maker – like her friends. Stevius Maximus and Andius Minimus were definitely at war with those three, but avoided battles as Davie and Mikey both had big fists which they often used to their advantage in the school playground.

"Why on earth did they put the poor girl next to Rosie?" Stevie muttered.

Andy shrugged his shoulders.

"Perhaps they thought a new girl would calm Rosie down a bit."

"A job for the legion," Stevie said. "To protect her."

Mrs Kerr addressed the class: "Good morning, children! I hope you all enjoyed yourselves over the break."

"Good morning, Mrs Kerr," chanted everyone in the class. Everyone, that is, but Rosie, Davie and Mikey.

"Today we have a new girl with us: Maisie Wu. Maisie comes all the way from China and I'm sure you'll all make her feel very welcome at our school here in Peebles. Good morning to you, Maisie."

"Good morning, Maisie," the class chanted together. Except, of course, Rosie, Davie and Mikey. In fact, Rosie just glowered rudely at Maisie, and looked the other way. Maisie smiled at the class, and Stevie loved to see her smile. She looked so cute. But he felt really embarrassed to see Rosie behave as she did…and worse was yet to come. It was obvious that Maisie's spoken English wasn't very good, although she seemed to understand perfectly well. Soon it became apparent that the red-nosed girl sitting next to Maisie wasn't going to help her in any way. When little Maisie asked Rosie a question in her broken English the other girl stuck her tongue out, after making sure that Mrs Kerr wasn't watching, and then looked away. That was bad enough, but what happened at play-time really made Stevie realise the legionaries would *have* to protect Maisie.

The little Chinese girl was standing alone, quietly minding her own business, when Crazy Davie, coaxed by his two friends, sidled up to her.

"Chinese, Japanese, don't forget to wash your knees!" he taunted.

Rosie sniggered unkindly, and poor Maisie looked both hurt and puzzled. She realised Davie was being unfriendly, but his Borders accent was so strong she hadn't a clue what he was talking about.

"Hey, Rosie," Mikey chipped in. "D'ya ken what? My dad says they live in caves in China, and that they're so poor they eat slugs and things!"

"Yuk!" said Rosie, sticking her tongue out at little Maisie yet again.

Maisie just stood there, bravely trying to ignore the three tormentors, but she looked so sad. Stevie wanted very much to see the girl smile again. He was about to go up to her when Mrs Kerr, who was in the playground, spotted what was happening, and went over to Maisie. The three delinquents ran off.

"Maisie, come and meet Amy," she said to the girl.

Maisie still looked sad as she was led across the playground and introduced to a fresh-faced blond girl.

"That's good!" Stevie said to Andy. "I like Amy."

Andy looked at Stevie in a funny way. Actually Andy liked Amy very much indeed but hadn't dared tell his friend.

Soon, Maisie was chatting with Amy and she was smiling. Her smile gave Stevie the courage he needed.

"Shall we?" Stevius Maximus asked Andius Minimus. "We have our duty to perform!"

"Aye!" replied Andius Minimus, only too keen to find an excuse to talk to Amy.

They high-fived together and marched across the playground to where Amy and Maisie stood talking.

"Er…" said Stevie.

Maisie looked round and smiled at him. It made him feel so warm and good inside. "Um…er…I'm Stevie. Stevie Scott. Happy to meet you, Maisie."

"Me happy too," said Maisie, still smiling at Stevie.

"Oh, and…er…this is Andy."

Maisie and Amy both smiled at Andy. Andy puffed himself up a bit. Amy had never smiled at him like that before!

"Um, China," Stevie continued. "Is it a long way off? Um…er…I know it's a long way off, but did it take long? I mean to get here from China? By plane, that is."

Maisie laughed. Stevie liked to hear her laugh.

"Rong time," she replied.

"Wrong?" Stevie queried. "Oh, a *long* time! Yeah, a long time. That's cool, Maisie."

And so the legionaries, feeling more relaxed by the minute, talked on with Maisie and Amy whilst other kids were rushing around in all directions. There was a lot of shouting and yelling going on, so the foursome found a quiet corner by the railings.

"What language do you speak at home?" Stevie asked of Maisie.

Stevie hadn't noticed Crazy Davie and his horrid friends creeping up behind him when he spoke.

"China speak many language," Maisie said. "Home speak Mandarin Chinese."

"Told you," Davie shouted loudly. "Duck language! Mandarins are ducks! My dad told me. We saw them in Edinburgh Zoo!"

At which Rosie and Mikey creased themselves with laughter and began quacking like ducks.

"Quack, quack!" echoed Crazy Davie, poking his ugly face right up close to Maisie.

"Clear off!" said Stevie, angrily. "Leave her alone!"

" 'Oh, leave the little Mandarin duck alone,' he says! Hey, Stevie, do you eat slugs too?"

"Shove off, Davie!" persisted Stevie.

He stood between Davie and Maisie, and somehow being near the girl made him feel brave. He *was* a legionary, after all, and it was his job to protect her.

"Who says, Chop Suey face? Try and make me!"

Davie knew how to show his aggression, and normally Stevius Maximus would have retreated rapidly, but the legionary stood his ground.

"Just be nice to her, can't you. She's a thousand times prettier to look at than Red-Nosed Rosie!"

Stevius Maximus was feeling very bold indeed, but there are things you should never say to someone like Davie, and calling his girlfriend 'Red-Nosed Rosie' was just one of those things. Davie's face suddenly turned very nasty – all sort of screwed-up looking – and he pushed Stevius Maximus backwards so hard that the legionary fell on to Maisie, whom he was supposed to protect, and she hit the railings. Maisie gave a little cry of distress, and Stevius Maximus turned to apologise to her.

Mistake number two! Never turn your back on the enemy. He had warned Andius Minimus about the dangers of doing this and yet he so wanted to say sorry to Maisie he couldn't stop himself. He felt two very painful punches in the back as both Davie and Mikey started to lay into him. This was too much for Stevius Maximus to bear. He turned round and thumped Crazy Davie as hard as he could on the chest.

"Say sorry to Maisie, or else!" he threatened the other boy.

"Stevie!" Andy tried to warn his friend, but it was too late. Stevius Maximus was no match against the flying fists of both Davie and Mikey, but he put up a very brave fight whilst Amy ran off to fetch Mrs Kerr from the other end of the playground. Andius Minimus did as he was told, and shielded Maisie, now crying, from the fray. Maisie was particularly upset when Stevius Maximus fell to the ground under a rain of punches, and Andius Minimus was trying to pull the two bullies away from his co-legionary when Mrs Kerr called out sharply. Crazy Davie, Muckle Mikey and Red-

Nosed Rosie ran off as Stevie painfully picked himself up from the ground.

"Hopelessly outnumbered," he mumbled to Andy, trying to cover up the shame he felt at being beaten up in front of Maisie.

"He started it!" Crazy Davie yelled at Mrs Kerr from a distance as she and Amy came up to Maisie and the two legionaries.

"Aye, he did too. I saw it!" affirmed Red-Nosed Rosie. "Stevie was threatening us and hit Davie really hard. Davie might be bruised for life now!"

Maisie just stood still, like a frightened rabbit, tears trickling down from her eyes.

"Stevie, you should be ashamed of yourself, fighting like that. You of all people! I'm afraid you're going to have to pay a little visit to Mr McKinnon. Okay?"

Stevie hung his head in shame, but felt better when Maisie said something that sounded like 'sheer-sheer', and stood up for him:

"Prease, no Stevie fault," she pleaded on his behalf. "Stevie kind. Stevie help Maisie."

"That's as it may be," said Mrs Kerr sternly. "But Stevie knows very well that there's to be no fighting in the playground!"

"Stay with her," Stevius Maximus commanded his co-legionary, and Andy was only too pleased to share this duty with Amy who put an arm around her new friend to comfort her.

Stevie marched off with pride to see Mr McKinnon, the headmaster, despite jeers from Davie and Mikey.

"Well, Stevie," said Mr McKinnon, "I must thank you for bringing to our attention the bad behaviour of three members of your class towards the new girl! We can't have teasing in *our* school! We had hoped that putting little Maisie next to Rosie might have made Rosie feel responsible towards her, but we obviously got it wrong. Mrs Kerr will be talking to the class. You're a good lad, Stevie, but in future don't fight back like that. Just come and let one of us know. Always tell a grown-up, Stevie, please!"

Stevie nodded, but he was *not* in agreement. It was *his* job as a legionary to put an end to that sort of thing.

After playtime, Mrs Kerr asked the class what they knew about China.

"They eat slugs and live in caves," Muckle Mikey shouted out.

"No, Mikey. They eat wonderful food, live in homes like our own and drive around in cars. But when people in *this* country lived in caves and ate things worse than slugs, the Chinese already had a great civilization and lived in fantastic palaces, wore fabulous clothes and had the best food you can imagine."

"Did they have Chinese restaurants and takeaways in China when people lived in caves here?" a little voice at the back called out.

Mrs Kerr laughed.

"I'm sure they did, Rory," she said. "And do you know they invented paper long ago in China, as well as printing, paper-money, silk, kite-flying, gun-powder and rockets?"

"Hey, cool!" said Rory.

"*And* the compass to help them navigate their ships. And why do we call plates, cups and saucers 'china'? Can anyone tell me?" Mrs Kerr asked the children.

Mikey's hand shot up.

"Because Chinese people have faces that look like plates!" he said, grinning stupidly.

"Go and see Mr McKinnon, Mikey," said Mrs Kerr. "I'm fed up with your rudeness. Amy, you tell us."

"Because it was invented in China as well," Amy said proudly. "Another name for it is por…pork…porky…, er…"

"Porcupine!" offered Mikey on his way to the door. Davie and Rosie sniggered.

"Porcelain, Amy. Good! But we usually just talk about the 'china', don't we? And there's so much else to learn about China. It's the third largest country in the world, for one thing, but has the largest population of any country. Do you know that one person out of every five in the world is Chinese? China is rapidly becoming one of the world's wealthiest countries because so many things are made in China. Just look at the labels on your toys, your clothes and many of the other things your parents buy. I'll bet you most of them will say 'Made in China'. And Chinese food is eaten and enjoyed around the whole world more than any other type of cooking. That's because people like it so much. Who's had food from our own Chinese restaurant here in Peebles?"

Everyone except for Davie and Rosie shot their hands up into the air.

"My Dad likes sweet and sour," one girl called out, "but I prefer spare ribs."

"No, I like chicken with cashew nuts best," another girl said. "It's yummy!"

"What about the noodles?" a small boy asked. "They're great!"

"They certainly are," said Mrs Kerr. "And of course Italian spaghetti originally came from China. A famous Italian explorer called Marco Polo brought many things like that back from China to Italy."

"Did he bring Polo mints back from China, Mrs Kerr?" a rather shy little girl queried.

"No, Debbie, I don't think Polo mints had anything to do with Marco Polo or with China. Now listen, all of you. If you're all really well-behaved this week, then next week we'll let you watch the movie 'Mulan'. It was Mr McKinnon's idea. Some of you may have seen it. It's about a Chinese princess from long ago."

After a few 'wows' and 'cools' all the children sat up straight to show their teacher how well-behaved they were. Everyone, that is, except for Crazy Davie and Red-Nosed Rosie.

At lunch-time Stevie, Andy, Amy and Maisie hung around together. There were, unfortunately, continued taunts from Crazy Davie and his pals who had now taken to pulling at the corners of their eyes, and turning them into narrow slits whenever they passed by little Maisie. Stevie thought this so stupid because Maisie's eyes were larger than Rosie's anyway, and a lot prettier!

"Just ignore them!" he said to the Chinese girl.

Over the lunch break Stevie learnt a lot about Maisie and about China. She sometimes had difficulty finding the right English word, and she often got her 'l's and her 'r's mixed up (she called the 'river' the 'liver'). However, he was able to converse with her perfectly well, and she told him that her father was a very clever scientist who was doing a 'P.H.D.' in

Edinburgh. Stevie nodded wisely, although he hadn't a clue what a 'P.H.D.' was, or how you 'do' one. He was minded to ask his dad, a doctor at the Borders General Hospital, when he got home. Until then he had an image of a 'P.H.D.' as an amazing instrument with all sorts of wires and tubes sticking out from it, and it could do *anything* you asked it to do, as long as you were clever enough to 'do' it. He learnt, with some delight, that the Wu family lived in a house very close to his own, and that the University had recommended Peebles to Maisie's dad as a good place for them to stay because the schools in the Borders were excellent. Every day, Mr Wu took the No. 62 bus up to Edinburgh to go to the University. Stevie was pleased to hear that the Wus would probably be in Scotland for three years or longer, but felt awful when Maisie said, "no rike school here. Want go back China!" She was close to tears again when she said this.

"Please don't go back to China yet," said Stevie. "We want you to stay with us."

He turned to Andy and Amy.

"We'll look after her, won't we?" he added. The others nodded.

"Look," continued Stevie. "Why don't you two girls join Andy and me for a special feast tomorrow morning, before school, in our Roman camp by the river. Just beyond the bridge. The camp's a secret really, but we can let you both in on it because we can trust you. Then you can see the baby ducks."

He turned and spoke to Andy.

"I was gonna tell you, Andius Minimus, but didn't get round to it. Too much legion business at playtime!"

Andy didn't need any persuading. He had always hoped Amy might join the legion one day. Unfortunately for him Amy shook her head.

"I'm sorry," she said. "I know my parents wouldn't allow it. They'd go spare. But *you* could go, Maisie."

"Go?" questioned Maisie, looking puzzled. She obviously thought she was being asked to go away.

"You could go with Stevie and Andy tomorrow morning to see the baby ducks."

"Ducklings," corrected Andy, trying to sound knowledgeable in front of Amy, but Amy just frowned at him.

"Ducklings *means* baby ducks," she explained to Maisie.

"Aye," said Stevie, turning to Maisie. "They're really cute. You'd love them. We'll bring some food. Real Roman food."

"Loman food? Duckling? Eat rike Peking duck?" she asked, looking a little worried.

Stevie laughed for he suddenly realised why Maisie looked worried.

"No, we don't *eat* the ducklings. Just look at them. Eat other food!" he explained to the girl.

"Ah! *Dui!*" she said, giggling. "No eat duckling!"

"Dway?" Stevie queried.

"Solly…" began Maisie, smiling at him.

"Sorry," Stevie corrected, kindly.

"So…ree!" Maisie repeated, giggling. "*Dui* Chinese. Mean 'yes'. Maisie understand. *See* duckling, *eat* other food. Loman food. Maisie rike feast."

"Like," Stevie corrected again. "L…L…L…this time!"

"Like, L…L…L…," echoed Maisie, laughing.

13

"So we'll see you outside your home at seven in the morning, then?" Stevie confirmed with Maisie. "We're Roman legionaries, so you'll be very safe."

"*Dui,*"the girl replied, smiling again.

After school Stevie and Andy waited with Maisie by the school gate until her mother turned up. Stevie thought the woman looked awfully young to be the girl's mother but, as he later found out, Chinese women tend to stay young-looking for a lot longer.

Stevie's parents would be no problem the following day. They were very easy-going, but he knew it might be more difficult for Andy to sneak out in the early morning. His big brother, Ross, always seemed to keep a beady eye trained on his little brother, although this was probably just as well, for Andy was forever getting himself into difficulties.

The next day Stevie stood by himself at the end of the path leading up to the Maisie's house. He had arrived early. Maisie must have spotted him from her window, for she soon appeared at the door, waving to him.

"*Ni hao!*" she called to Stevie as she came down the path.

Stevie looked at his knees, wondering if there was something wrong with them.

Maisie laughed.

"*Ni hao!*" she repeated, giggling. "Mean 'harro' in Chinese!"

"Oh, hallo!" said Stevie. "Is that Mandarin Chinese?"

"*Dui,*" replied Maisie, smiling prettily.

Stevie was really beginning to like Maisie very much. She was so bonny compared with the other girls in his class, although he did think that Amy had a nice face.

"Where's Andy?" Maisie asked.

Andy should certainly have arrived by then. He, too, was usually early. Stevie could only assume he had been delayed by Ross.

"We'll go on ahead," Stevie said to Maisie. "Andy'll join us when he's ready."

Stevie opened the poly-bag he was carrying to show Maisie its contents.

"Look!" he said, proudly pointing out the items of food in the bag.

"Carrots, apples and bread. Good Roman food!"

"Loman?"

Maisie had one of her puzzled expressions that made him laugh.

"Roman," he corrected. "R...R...R..."

"Roman, R...R...R...!" repeated Maisie.

"Look!" said Stevie.

He arched his back, to make himself look bigger, and then marched up and down a few times.

"Roman soldier. Me Roman soldier!" he said importantly, patting his chest.

Maisie's eyes opened wide with amusement, and then she covered her mouth with her hand and giggled.

"Funny!" she said. "Roman soldier funny!"

Stevie wasn't *supposed* to look funny, but he didn't mind because he liked to hear the girl laugh.

"Let's go!" he said, and Maisie followed him along the road, down the cut leading to the river, along the bank, past the bridge to where it was overgrown with long grass and nettles.

"Stay on the path, Maisie," Stevie advised. "Nettles! They sting. Ouch!"

Hopping about from one foot to the other, he showed the girl what it would feel like to be stung by nettles.

"Ouch!" mimicked Maisie, hopping about as well and laughing. She kept on saying 'ouch' and giggling to herself as she followed Stevie along the path to the Roman camp. The camp wasn't far at all. It was beside a large willow where the grass and weeds had been trodden down and had turned brown. There was an old log there and a few large flat stones.

"Our Roman camp!" said Stevie, proudly indicating the spot with a wave of his hand.

"*Dui*," said Maisie. "Roman soldier eat here." She looked serious.

"You've got it!" exclaimed Stevie happily. He told Maisie to sit on the log, for that was where important people sat, and Stevie sat on one of the stones and opened his poly-bag.

"Here," he said, "have a Roman carrot."

"Roman carrot!" Maisie repeated.

Soon the children were gnawing away at carrots and munching red apples before finishing their feast with dry unbuttered bread. Stevie explained that this was how the Romans ate their bread when he saw Maisie holding the slice of bread and just staring at it with a puzzled expression.

"They didn't have butter, you see," he said.

"Romans no butter," Maisie said, frowning, and then she giggled. After the bread they shared a can of Fanta orange.

Suddenly Stevie went still. He held up his hand.

"Shhh!" he cautioned, although the girl hadn't actually said anything.

"Ah!" gasped Maisie quietly, pointing ahead of her. A train of ducks had just waddled into view along the river bank in front of them. There was a proud mother duck followed by five fluffy little ducklings. Stevie loved to see the entranced expression on Maisie's pretty face. The mother duck, and then her offspring, one by one, squatted on the verge and slipped out of sight down the sloping bank into the water. There was a funny plopping sound as each duckling hit the water below. Soon they had all disappeared from view, but the children could still hear the mother duck's loud, bossy quacks and her little ducklings' high-pitched, excited quacks.

"Here," said Stevie, slowly rising from his stone seat. "Come closer. You can see them in the water."

He went very carefully through the long grass to the edge of the steep bank and peered down.

"They're really cute, Maisie. You should see them swimming about."

Maisie held back.

"No near water," she said nervously. "*Baba* say no."

"Baba?"

Stevie looked back at Maisie.

"*Baba*," she repeated. "Mean father in Chinese," the girl explained.

"Oh, like Papa," said Stevie. "Look it's quite safe, Maisie. I'll hold on to you. You'll be fine," he reassured her.

There was obviously a struggle going on in Maisie's mind between her eagerness to see the ducklings in the water and her duty to obey her father. Finally, curiosity got the better of her. She had seen baby ducklings in cages in the market in China,

but never free, in the wild, like this. Slowly she arose from the log and walked gingerly towards Stevie. He held out his hand for her to grab on to. She peered down at the ducklings from the bank as she reached for Stevie's hand.

What really happened next Stevie never found out for it was all so quick. Maisie seemed to stumble, possibly on a large stone hidden in the long grass. Suddenly she disappeared over the bank before Stevie had a chance to catch hold of her. She splashed into the river face first. Initially Stevie thought this was some sort of joke on Maisie's part, and he gave a nervous little laugh. But she was fully clothed, and was splashing around a lot. Then she disappeared. One...two...three seconds went by, and she failed to resurface. An awful panic engulfed Stevie. What if Maisie couldn't swim? He hadn't even asked her that simple question. Of course! Now he realised why her father had told her not to go near the water. The girl was drowning in the River Tweed and it was all his fault. If only Andy was with him now. Andy, and his big brother Ross. But Stevie was there on his own, and poor Maisie was drowning!

CHAPTER 2: THE UNHAPPY DRAGON

Stevie kicked off his shoes and dived into the water. As he did so he thought he heard someone shouting from further along the bank. He was a strong swimmer, and spotted Maisie straightaway. She was flailing about under the water, and bubbles were coming from her mouth. There was a terrified expression on her poor little face. Stevie made a grab for the girl, but her frantic arms and legs kept pushing him away. He repeatedly tried to get hold of her body from behind, unsuccessfully. Soon he became very disorientated, and he really wasn't sure which way was up and which was down. Then Maisie floated past him. She had gone very still and seemed almost peaceful in the water, her eyes closed and her black hair drifting about her face. He took a firm hold of her body as he tried to work out which way was up. He saw a light and swam strongly towards this, holding on to Maisie. The girl seemed almost weightless. Like a fairy, he thought, not that he had ever pulled a *real* fairy along under water. The light became brighter and brighter, and suddenly his head broke above the surface. He was gasping for air, but he wasted no time in getting breath for himself. He immediately pushed Maisie's head above the water, opened her mouth and with his arms around her chest squeezed all the water from her. He pulled her safely out and up the bank on to her side. Stevie was just so relieved when Maisie started to cough and splutter. He patted her back. The girl made a few croaky noises, then very quickly came to.

"I'm so sorry, I'm so sorry!" Stevie kept saying.

"No Stevie fault," said Maisie, looking up at him. "Maisie no swim. Bad girl. Disobey *Baba*."

"No, Maisie. I shouldn't have tried to persuade you."

Maisie smiled at Stevie.

"Wanted see ducklings swim. Maisie fault. Maybe now see!"

Maisie turned her head to look for the ducklings and then screamed. Stevie looked back at the river to see why she had screamed, and froze in horror. There *was* no river, for they were lying on the bank of an enormous lake.

"Stevie!" Maisie gasped, turning again to look at the boy. "I think we're deaded. Drownded!"

Stevie quickly felt for the pulse at his wrist, just as his father had taught him to do. He breathed a sigh of relief. He felt for Maisie's pulse, and it too was strong, although a little fast.

"No, Maisie," he reassured her. "It's okay. You're not deaded – I mean dead."

Stevie looked at that lake again. On the other side of the lake were mountains, far higher than the hills around Peebles. To the left was an island and on this island were several strange-looking buildings with funny, curvy roofs, and some people in long cloaks. He stood up and looked over the top of the bank.

"Oh my God!" he said quietly. He was looking at a town of low, wooden buildings and dusty streets. There were no cars. Only carts and horses. The people wore the oddest of garments, but the most extraordinary thing was that they appeared to be

Chinese. Initially he had wondered if they had somehow floated downstream to Berwick-upon-Tweed, but now he realised he was in a very alien place indeed. Maisie had also stood up and was staring at these people with Stevie. The boy saw that she was trembling, and he put his arm around her to comfort her. It was then that he noticed she was dressed very differently. Instead of her pale blue school sweater and black skirt she was wearing a beautiful, silky red dress which came down almost to her feet, and it had extra long sleeves that dangled from her wrists to the ground. Her hair was different, too. She no longer had it tied back in a pony-tail. Instead it was loose about her shoulders.

"Your dress, Maisie. How come it's different?"

"Silk dance dress," Maisie said, looking down at her dress, and she raised her arms in the air to show him the long trailing sleeves. "Have Chinese dance dresses like this at home. Feel!"

Stevie ran his fingers over the silk. He loved the smooth texture.

"Stevie!" Maisie exclaimed. "Look at self!"

Stevie looked down at his own clothes. Instead of school clothes he was dressed in a loose white shirt and wide white trousers that came to just below his knees. On his feet were open sandals.

Maisie was looking very worried. She began to cry, and Stevie held her close.

"Stevie, we *must* be deaded," she sobbed. "This place Hangzhou. My home in China. In China say deaded people go back home place."

"But *I* don't come from Han...Hang..."

"Hangzhou."

"No, I don't, and you've got a pulse so you can't be deaded. I mean dead. *I* should know because my dad's a doctor."

Maisie turned and pointed to the lake.

"See," she said. "West Lake. Island there with shrine. Beyond lake, mountain with many temple. This Hangzhou. But no motor-boat on lake. No car in town and no big building. This like Hangzhou long time ago. My *Kung-Kung,* he live in Hangzhou, but not this Hangzhou."

"*Kung-Kung?*" Stevie queried.

"Grand man?" sobbed Maisie.

"Grand man?" Stevie wasn't sure what she meant.

"Father of mother. Miss very much, my grand man," repeated Maisie.

"Oh! Grandfather! Your grandfather lives here. Well, here as it is now, and not then as it was where we are...now?" Stevie felt *very* confused. He pinched himself to see whether he was dreaming, only a little too hard.

"Ouch!" he yelped.

Maisie laughed through her tears.

"Ouch!" she repeated. "Like when go Roman camp."

"*Ni hao!*"

Stevie looked at his knees, but they seemed okay. Then he realised it wasn't Maisie speaking, and he remembered from earlier on that '*ni hao*' meant 'hallo' in Chinese.

"Who said that?" he asked, staring at Maisie who looked equally puzzled.

"I didn't say '*that*'! I said '*ni hao*'!"

It was the same voice.

Stevie looked around hoping to see Andy or Ross or someone else he knew, but all that he could see close by was a large white bird standing at the top of the lakeside bank.

"*Ni hao!*" came the voice again. This time Stevie saw that it was the bird itself who spoke. Its beak moved, and the words came out from its beak. At first he felt too surprised to say anything, but after Maisie bowed politely to the bird and said '*ni hao*' back to it Stevie did the same.

Maisie spoke in Chinese to the bird, a huge white crane.

"What did you just say?" Stevie asked her.

"Tell my name and ask 'have you eaten?'" she replied.

"Why did you ask if the bird has just eaten?" enquired Stevie, perplexed.

"In China polite ask this when grown-ups meet."

"I didn't hear you tell him *your* name, Maisie."

"Tell Chinese name. Hua-Mei. Mean…"

Maisie looked embarrassed.

"Mean 'Pretty Flower'. Friends in China usually call me Mei."

Stevie looked at his new friend and thought the name 'Pretty Flower' suited her very much.

"Can I call you Mei, too?" he asked.

"*Dui.*"

Mei smiled at him.

"And this one?"

It was the White Crane again, speaking in English.

"Speaks that funny language, doesn't he!"

"It's not a funny language," objected Stevie. "It's English!"

"Sounds funny to me. Like ducks quacking! Jade Emperor told me to learn it before meeting you kids! Took me at least ten minutes, you know. Anyway, what's *your* name?" the crane asked Stevie.

"Stevie. Stevie Scott, from Peebles."

White Crane looked at Stevie and shrugged his wings.

"What does it mean? Stevie? Doesn't sound like a *real* name to me! Might as well be called 'Blob' or 'Thing'."

"Of course it's a real name! It's *my* name! There are other Stevies in Peebles too. Why should it *mean* anything? It's me! Why…?"

Stevie was beginning to get cross, and he resented the idea of being called either 'Blob' or 'Thing', but he felt a gentle pinch on his arm. It was Mei. The look on her face suggested to him that he should let her do the talking.

"Mr Crane," she said politely in English, "maybe you help find new name for Stevie."

"I don't…" Stevie began, but stopped when the girl gave him another little pinch.

"I can't, Pretty Flower," said the crane. "You see, I'm not good at names. Not at all good. But I know someone who is."

The crane pointed with a wing at the figure of an old man dressed in a white garment, squatting by the roadside at the edge of the town. He was slurping up noodles from a bowl, using chopsticks.

"I'll introduce you," White Crane added, and the children followed him along the bank to meet the man.

"*Ni hao*," the old fellow said, looking up at the children as they approached. "Have you eaten?"

Stevie remembered what Mei had told him.

"Er… yes. Actually, we had a Roman breakfast. In Peebles."

The man nodded. It seemed pointless to Stevie to ask whether the fellow himself had eaten whilst he was still enjoying a bowl of noodles.

"Peebles, eh? Hmm! That's west of here, isn't it? Yes, The Jade Emperor's messenger told me all about you two children. *And your task.*"

"Our task?"

Stevie and Mei looked at one another.

"Later, children." He stood up and bowed. "I'm Mr White."

Mei gasped. She bowed *very* respectfully.

"Preased to meet you, Mr White. I'm…"

"Yes, Pretty Flower, I know who you are. But your friend, we must find a proper name for him. He comes from the west, so we'll call him 'White Tiger'."

Mei turned and smiled at Stevie.

"*Ni hao*, White Tiger," she said.

Stevie liked the name. It made him feel strong and important. But like Mei he really just wanted to get back to Peebles, and he realised that they were already late for school.

"Mr White, can you tell us how to get back to Peebles?" he asked.

"I'm sorry, I can't…but I know someone who can. The problem is he's in no fit state to tell you, he's so unhappy! That's why you're both here, of course. That's why the Jade Emperor sent for you. To make him happy again."

White Tiger and Mei looked at each other.

"Who?" they asked together.

"Don't they know?" Mr White asked White Crane.

"Well, not really. Not actually *know*. We hadn't got beyond the name bit, you see."

Mr White explained:

"*He* is the Blue Dragon, children. Very depressed, he's been, since the Monkey King stole his magical staff and his red pearl. You see, he needs these things to bring on the rain for the farmers and to help their crops to grow. And when the mischievous Monkey King stole them he left his river and crawled into a cave in the mountain and he won't come out. Says he's too ashamed, and his beloved Red Phoenix bird has flown south again because she got fed up with his moodiness. It's all going horribly wrong, but the Jade Emperor has every confidence in you two children. He's sure you can put things right."

Stevie hadn't a clue what Mr White was talking about, or who the Jade Emperor was, but it was looking as though their only chance of ever getting back to Peebles lay with the Blue Dragon in his cave. It all sounded a bit scary, but then he looked at Mei and he suddenly felt brave. He had to get the girl back to her parents in Peebles. He just had to!

"How...?" he began to ask Mr White.

"Oh, White Crane will see to that!" the old man interrupted, squatting down and resuming his breakfast of noodles.

"I think we should leave him now," White Crane said to the children. "He's got a job to do looking after this city."

White Tiger glanced at Mei.

"Mr White," she explained. "Old god of Hangzhou City. Legend. Mr White look after city by day. Mr Black at night."

"God?" questioned White Tiger, not believing his ears.

"*Dui!*" the girl replied, smiling.

White Tiger looked back at the old man tucking into his bowl of noodles.

"A god? Him?"

"Shhh!" said Mei, holding a finger to her lips.

"And the Jade Emperor? Who's he?" White Tiger asked.

Mei was just about to say something when White Crane called out to the children.

"Well," he said impatiently, "are you coming or not? The mournful old Blue Dragon might drown in his tears if we don't get there soon!"

Suddenly Mei gasped. White Crane had just spread out his beautiful white wings.

"Oh, Mr Crane! Prease show me 'White Crane Spread Wings'."

"Not you *too!*" White Crane said in an exasperated sort of way. "Boring, boring!"

Then he lifted one foot off the ground and stood with his wings stretched out wide.

"I do get fed up with people asking me to do this, you know," he added.

"White Crane spread wings," Mei explained to White Tiger. "Famous *Tai-Chi* move. *Baba* teach me *Tai-Chi*. Do together every morning – but not today," she added sadly. "Miss *Baba* so much!"

"What's *Tai-Chi?*" asked White Tiger.

"Many Chinese do," replied Mei. "Slow martial art. More like dance. Help control body and mind."

"Martial art?" questioned White Tiger. "Like Kung Fu?" He

had seen an old Bruce Lee movie on the telly, and remembered the bodies flying around all over the place. Mei laughed.

"No," she said. "Mei show!"

At which Mei gave a beautiful demonstration of *Tai-Chi*, with its graceful movements, including 'White Crane Spreads Its Wings'. It looked very gentle to White Tiger. Not a bit like the Bruce Lee movie. He would have liked her to go on, but White Crane was getting *very* grumpy.

"Okay," grumbled the great bird. "So I *am* a bit out of practice. That's why you're better than me. But we really must get going."

"How?" asked White Tiger.

"Work it out, Mr Clever Head!"

Oh dear, thought White Tiger. He really *is* in a bad mood now.

"Where Brue Dragon?" asked Mei sweetly, smiling at White Crane who softened on seeing her smile.

"Oh, near Tai Shan, Shandong province," the crane replied politely.

"Where's that?" asked White Tiger.

"*That* is at least a thousand *li* away!"

White Crane sounded grumpy again.

"What's a *li*?" White Tiger whispered to Mei.

"About third of mile," she whispered back. "Old-fashioned Chinese measurement."

"So?" persisted the crane, glaring at White Tiger. "Are you going to get on or not?"

"On what?" White Tiger asked. White Crane was beginning to make *him* feel irritable too.

"Not awfully bright, is he? Can't think why the Jade Emperor chose him!" the crane said to Mei.

"I..." White Tiger began to protest crossly, but he felt a further gentle pinch from his new friend.

"White Tiger velly clever. Velly brave. You see!"

Then she turned to White Tiger who felt a lot better after hearing her kind words about him.

"You go first. In front."

"Where? What?" he asked, beginning to feel flummoxed.

"On Mr Crane's back," the girl replied. "He take us to Shandong."

White Tiger glanced nervously at the White Crane.

"A thousand *li*?" he queried, trying to look brave. "On that thing...er...I mean on Mr Crane's back?"

Mei nodded and smiled one of her smiles. Suddenly White Tiger felt much braver. He climbed onto the back of the large crane and Mei climbed up behind him, putting her arms around his waist. White Tiger liked that. It made him feel important. He put his own arms around the slender neck of the huge bird, the crane spread its wings again and they were lifted off the ground and up into the air. They went higher and higher and faster and faster. Soon they were travelling at an incredible speed as the crane rhythmically beat its huge wings up and down. The sweep of the bird's wings seemed measured and gentle, and yet they were going so fast. White Tiger couldn't understand why, but he didn't want to risk upsetting the crane by asking him. He looked down at the ground way below. There were watery, strip-like fields and many tiny figures with wide-brimmed, conical hats, bent down doing

things in the fields. He turned to face Mei. From the ecstatic expression on her face she was clearly enjoying the ride. He asked her what the people were doing down there and she told him those were 'lice' fields.

Lice…? he thought

Suddenly he shouted back at Mei.

"Rice, Mei, rice! R…R…R!"

Mei laughed.

"Rice, R…R…R!" she shouted back.

"Mei?"

"*Dui!*"

"Who's the Jade Emperor, Mei?

White Tiger hoped the crane hadn't heard him ask the question.

"Jade Emperor luler of heaven."

"Ruler?"

"*Dui*. Different emperor on earth. My *Kung-Kung* teach me these things. Teach many things. Miss him very much in Peebles, my *Kung-Kung*."

Mei looked sad, as though she might cry.

"I've an idea, Mei. When we get home ask your mum to arrange for your *Kung-Kung* to come to Scotland. To Peebles!"

He didn't want Mei to have *any* excuse to go back to China – well, modern China – when they returned to Peebles.

Mei smiled instantly.

"See!" she exclaimed. "White Tiger clever! Like Mei tell Mr Crane."

White Tiger felt exceedingly happy as they sped through the sky towards Shandong, looking down at the busy people in the rice fields, at winding paths, small villages and larger towns. Everywhere there seemed to be people, and he remembered what Mrs Kerr had said about China now having more people in it than any other country. And yet, despite this, it looked so very peaceful down there.

Suddenly White Tiger spotted what appeared to be three white aircraft approaching them.

"Aeroplanes," he said excitedly to Mei. "Look!"

"*Feiji?*" the girl questioned. "No. Birds."

Mei was right. Three white cranes, just like the one they were sitting on, were coming towards them at an amazing speed. White Crane turned his head and spoke to White Tiger. He seemed to be in a better humour.

"The three Crane Maidens," he explained, calling out "*Ni hao!*" as the cranes sped by.

"Maidens?" queried White Tiger.

"Yep! Come down from heaven to bathe in a lake and when they take off their magical clothes they turn into beautiful maidens. Trouble is, one of them is really upset. See, once, as a maiden, she fell in love with a mortal man. He hid her magical clothes. They even married and had a son called Zhang. Then his mother found her clothes. Made her put them on again and she turned back into a bird. Like me. She never saw her husband or her boy again."

The White Crane chuckled, but Mei said it was a very sad story.

"Lose husband and son! *Poor* Crane maiden!" she called out.

White Tiger felt more like asking the White Crane some questions now.

"Mr Crane, how are we supposed to help the Blue Dragon?"

"By getting his magical staff and red pearl back, of course. From the Monkey King!"

White Tiger didn't dare ask how on earth they were going to do that, but he needed some reassurance that this whole exercise would get them back to Peebles. He still felt guilty about Mei falling into the River Tweed, and desperately wanted to return her to her parents.

"The Blue Dragon? He'll be able to get us back to Peebles if we retrieve those things for him, won't he?"

"Oh, there's no telling what Blue Dragon will or won't do. All depends on his mood at the time."

"Mr Crane?"

The White Crane sighed.

"Yes, White Tiger? You're nearly as bad for asking questions as the immortals I have to carry about. Still, this does make a change, I suppose. And those immortals can get a bit heavy."

"Immortals?"

"Yeah! From the island of Penglai. Kind of magical place with crystal palaces and pearls growing on trees, and it floats about on the back of a huge turtle. Trouble is the turtle can be a bit slow, so if they want to go somewhere quickly they call me. Eight of them, there are. Lucky number in this place, eight. Anyway, I jumped at it when the Jade Emperor's messenger asked if I could help out carrying a couple of children. Didn't expect so many questions, though! So?"

"What?" asked White Tiger.

"Your next question?"

"Oh, I just wondered how long it was going to take to get to the Blue Dragon's cave."

"Just over there!" said the White Crane. "The big mountain in the distance is Tai Shan, the holy mountain of the east. Blue Dragon has taken refuge on that little mountain to the left. Not much of a cloud on it today, so he must be *very* depressed!"

The crane looked round at White Tiger, and the boy was sure he could see a smile on the bird's face – if, that is, birds *can* smile.

"Five minutes. Prepare for landing!"

White Tiger gripped the crane's neck more tightly.

"Hey, don't strangle me. It's a long drop from up here, you know!"

Soon they came in to land on a rocky ledge. There was a pool of water, fed by several streams trickling out from a large cave at the far end.

"Oh dear!" exclaimed the White Crane as the children scrambled down off his back. "That dragon's got it really bad. He's going to lose a lot of water with all that crying. Not good for dragons to lose water."

"I thought dragons breathed fire and stuff!" said White Tiger.

Mei enlightened him by explaining that in China dragons lived in water and breathed out clouds to make rain for the farmers. They were *always* good. Not at all like their European cousins, thought White Tiger.

"Well, children, I have to leave you now. Keep teaching your friend, Pretty Flower. I suppose he's not really that bad. Better than an immortal, anyway. Till we meet again, *Zai jian!*"

"Mean goodbye in Chinese," whispered Mei.

"*Zai jian!*" the children called together.

"*Xie xie!*" added Mei.

White Tiger remembered hearing the girl say this (pronounced 'sheer sheer') after he had stood up for her against Crazy Davie and his friends. She explained that it means 'thank you' in Chinese.

White Crane flapped his wings, lifting himself off the edge of the cliff before soaring up into the sky.

White Tiger and Mei looked at each other.

"I'll go first," said White Tiger pointing at the dark entrance to the dragon's cave. Even if Chinese dragons *were* supposed to be good rather than bad he couldn't bear the thought of any more harm coming to his friend. "Just stay close behind me."

The children entered the cave. It was very dim and smelt a bit like the woods near Peebles after the rain. The weirdest thing, however, was the noise coming from within the dark cave. It wasn't a scary noise, but it was awfully mournful. White Tiger thought it sounded a bit like a cow being sick – that is, if cows ever *were* sick. He didn't really know. Just listening to the sound made him feel sad, and he noticed that Mei's eyes had gone watery.

"Poor Brue Dragon," she said. "Must help him!"

As White Tiger's eyes grew accustomed to the low light he began to make out a shape at the side of the great cave, huddled up against the wall. It was dark bluish, and there was a rim of triangular scales outlining its humpy back. White Tiger's gaze followed the scales to a long twisting tail, most of which lay hidden in the pool of water surrounding the Blue Dragon. His eyes then traced the scales in the opposite direction to the

beast's long neck which was flopped onto the cave floor and partly submerged by water. Beyond this, peeping above the water, was the top half of the dragon's enormous blue head. The head itself was the size of a cow. There were two cow-like horns sticking out from its brow and it was immersed in water up to its large nostrils. Every time the dragon breathed out, little wavelets spread from these nostrils across the pool and the cave echoed with the muffled sobs of the unhappy beast. From where the children stood, one plate-like eye could be seen, and it was half-covered with a leathery fold that looked more like a small blind than an eyelid. From the corner of this eye a constant stream of water trickled into the pool. The Blue Dragon must have heard the splash of the water as they waded towards him.

"Oh dear," he moaned in a very deep voice. "Is that you, Pretty Flower and White Tiger? I'm so *very* sad, you know. And it's all because of that mischievous monkey. Do say you can help me. Please, please say you can help. The Jade Emperor's messenger promised you could. Said you'd been sent for especially to help get back those things the nasty monkey thief stole from me. If you can't help me then I may never see my beloved Red Phoenix again. Boo-hoo!" sobbed the Blue Dragon.

Mei showed no fear at all of the enormous creature. She sploshed her way through the pool of dragon tears right up to its vast blue head, reached up with her small hand and patted the dragon just above his nostrils.

"No worry, Mr Dragon," she said, gently. "White Tiger velly clever. Velly brave. He get Brue Dragon's things back. Pretty Flower promise this too."

Mei's words made White Tiger feel good, but he just hoped he could fulfil her promise to the dragon. The dragon blinked his leathery eyelid at the little Chinese girl.

"He will?" he asked. "Get back my red pearl and magical staff?"

"Mmm!" said Mei, stroking the dragon's nose.

"Feel better already," the dragon said. "Your red dress, though. It reminds me of my lovely Red Phoenix. You see, I can't hold my head up until I get my magical pearl and staff back. I feel too ashamed. The Monkey King comes here, and I treat him like royalty, and he goes and tricks me and brings so much shame down on me that I've had to crawl into this miserable cave and hide myself. It's enough to make you want to weep!"

The Blue Dragon didn't seem to realise he had already produced a veritable flood of tears.

"And how can I now promise rain and a good harvest for the farmers without those things, eh?" the Blue Dragon continued. "There's the dragon boat festival coming up soon, and I can't do that without my staff. And the dragon dance next year. How can I do *that* without my red pearl? And all the wretched thief does with my staff is to use it for fighting. He only stole the pearl to make himself rich! It makes things multiply, you see. That's why the farmers need it after planting. He, that monkey thief, just makes money multiply with it. The people can't eat money, can they? I just feel like sobbing," he moaned, the tears now flooding from his huge eyes.

White Tiger felt rather sceptical about the Blue Dragon's ability to get them back to Peebles, but he thought he had to arrange *some* sort of deal with the beast. After all, if he and Mei were going to take risks getting those things for him, surely the dragon could promise to help them afterwards!

"Okay, Mr Blue Dragon," he said. "We'll try our best to get those things back for you. But then could you possibly…?"

"No, no, no!" groaned the dragon. "Can't do! Not now, please."

White Tiger was beginning to feel a bit fed up with the dragon, but Mei continued to stroke the beast soothingly on the nose. Then she stood on tip-toes and whispered something into the dragon's floppy ear.

"What did you say to him?" White Tiger asked as the dragon continued to sob.

"Say 'dear powerful dragon, we your friends. Trust White Tiger.'"

"Oh dear," said White Tiger, sounding rather like the dragon himself. "I don't know where to begin!"

"You could try the beginning," offered the dragon who suddenly fixed White Tiger with his large eye. "Pan Gu?"

"Pan Gu?" White Tiger hadn't a clue what the dragon was talking about.

"Pan Gu. He made heaven and earth. *That* was the beginning!"

White Tiger couldn't for the life of him see where this was getting them.

"Then came the goddess, Nu Wa," continued the Blue Dragon slowly. "She made the first people from mud, you know!"

White Tiger felt a bit muddy on the outside by now, but he was sure he wasn't muddy inside.

"Then there was the water buffalo god, Shen Nong. Sad story, that one. Made one mistake and the Jade Emperor said he would have to spend the rest of eternity on earth working away for all the farmers."

"Poor water buffalo god," said Mei. "Sad for him!"

"Yes," said the dragon. "It almost brings tears to your eyes, it does! And then that Monkey King comes along and tries to make himself immortal. Caused all sorts of troubles in heaven. They even put him in jail, you know. But he broke out. They told me this after he'd stolen my things! Enough to make you weep, it is. Even Lord Buddha is angry with him."

Mei's eyes lit up at the mention of the Buddha.

"Mr Dragon Buddhist?" she asked the miserable Blue Dragon.

"Oh, I'm just me!" he replied. "And a very unhappy me at that."

"My *Kung-Kung* Buddhist," the girl said. "Teach me many things about Lord Buddha. Say 'let go what you want – find happy then.'"

"Oh, Pretty Flower, I can't let go. You see, it's bad enough only having four claws instead of five, like the golden imperial dragons, but to be a blue dragon without his staff and pearl, it's just, well...I could almost cry, you know!"

Tears streamed from his large sad eyes, and the pool in the cave was getting deeper.

"Mr Dragon," Mei said, tenderly rubbing the dragon's nose. "Prease no cry so much. Just tell White Tiger where can find bad Monkey King."

The Blue Dragon looked at Mei.

"I do like your red dress, Pretty Flower," he said. "But that red, you know, it so reminds me of my Red Phoenix bird, and *that* makes me feel rather tearful!"

"Mr Dragon! No so miserable! Prease! Where Monkey King?"

"Oh, here, there and everywhere!"

"What mean, Mr Dragon?"

For the first time Mei seemed almost cross.

"Look, he can somersault over the clouds," replied the dragon. "They say he can clear three thousand *li* in one jump. It's a case of 'now you see him, now you don't' sort of thing, if you get my drift."

Mei was frowning, but White Tiger suddenly thought of something.

"Mr Dragon, you said Monkey King wants to be immortal. He must be looking for something somewhere that'll *make* him immortal. Surely *that's* where we'll find him!"

Mei looked proudly at White Tiger.

The Blue Dragon's eyelid dropped right down, and he seemed to be lost in thought for a while.

"Mr Dragon," continued White Tiger, "White Crane told me about the eight immortals on Penglai. How do *they* stay immortal?"

Mei looked *very* proudly at White Tiger.

"Why, the magical peaches in the garden of the Queen Mother of the West, of course!" the dragon replied, its large eyelid suddenly flicking open. "Everyone knows that!"

"Well," persisted White Tiger, "that's where…"

"Um…" interrupted the dragon, "er…well…per…"

"Yes?" the children said together, eagerly.

"… maybe…"

"What?"

"…HAPS!" roared the Blue Dragon, suddenly lifting his huge head out of the water. The children almost fell over in surprise.

"I've an idea!" he exclaimed. "Why don't you two go to the garden of the Queen Mother of the West? If the peaches are turning ripe then the Monkey King is bound to come and try to steal one!"

Mei smiled at White Tiger and he winked at her.

"And how do we get there, please?" White Tiger asked.

"Silly question!" the dragon answered. "Go west of course!"

"Right!" said White Tiger, grinning at Mei.

"No!" said the dragon. "Left! I'm sure you have to turn left outside this awful cave to go west. Just look at the sun and see which way the Jun bird takes it."

"Jun bird?"

Mei helped White Tiger out.

"Old Chinese story," she explained. "My *Kung-Kung* tell me. Once ten suns. Each day a black bird called Jun bird take one sun across sky east to west. Ten Jun birds take turn. One day all ten birds take suns out together. Ten suns! World get very hot. Houses start burning. So Emperor of Heaven send famous archer called Yi to fix problem. Yi shoot dead nine Jun birds so just one sun left. Yi save world, but Jade Emperor angry. Say shouldn't kill other nine Jun birds. Just wound. So Yi no go back heaven. Stay on earth and marry."

"Oh!" said White Tiger, feeling confused by the story. Meanwhile the Blue Dragon was starting to look anxious again.

"No worry, Mr Dragon" Mei said. "We go west. Find Monkey King. White Tiger get staff and pearl for Brue Dragon."

The dragon looked at the girl.

"You will be careful of the black tortoise, won't you?" he warned.

"Who's he?" asked White Tiger.

"Oh, just a very bad tortoise. Comes from the north and enjoys fighting."

"Sounds like Crazy Davie to me," White Tiger joked, and Mei giggled.

"And the *gui*!" added the dragon. "Take extra care if the *gui* appear."

"The what?" asked White Tiger. He didn't like the sound of the *gui*.

"Restless ghosts, they are. If you give them food they might go away. *If* you're very lucky. If not, they'll probably steal your bodies. They're particularly fond of children, you see. "

"They'll what?"

White Tiger didn't like the sound of the *gui* one little bit.

"Mmm," replied the dragon. "But I've prepared two bags of food for your journey. Should be enough for yourselves and the *gui*. Water too. My clouds are pretty pathetic at the moment, what with the way I'm feeling just now, but I can still make enough water for you to drink."

You can say that all right, thought White Tiger, up to his knees in water.

"The bags are there, by the entrance of this horrible cave!"

And so the children bade the unhappy Blue Dragon *zai jian*, and left the dingy cave to begin their journey west in the hope of finding the Monkey King and somehow retrieving the Blue Dragon's magical staff and red pearl. *Then* they might find out how to get back to Peebles!

CHAPTER 3: THE QILIN

Once they were down from the small mountain the children discovered there was a very pleasant path, winding between fields of corn, where men and women were working away despite the heat of the sun, and through small villages where little Chinese children would run up to them excitedly, calling "*ni hao, ni hao!*" One boy tugged at Mei's red dress and asked her something. She replied in Chinese.

"What did he ask?" enquired White Tiger.

"Ask if have present for him!" Mei laughed. "Mei say send present from Peebles!"

Soon they reached a broad river.

"This good," said Mei. "In China all livers go west to east. Just follow liver."

White Tiger smiled.

"River," he said kindly. "R...R...R."

Mei giggled and repeated "river, r...r...r."

"Well," said White Tiger. "Seems a good place to me to stop and have lunch. I'm starving!"

There were several rocks lying around, some small enough for them to sit on.

"*Xing!*" said Mei, putting her bag beside a rock just the right size for the two of them.

"Shing?" White Tiger queried.

Mei laughed.

"Mean okay!"

"Ah! *Xing!*" he repeated, sitting beside Mei and opening the dragon's food bag. In it were lots of little parcels of food neatly wrapped in leaves and tied with string. Also a ceramic bottle, with a stopper, full of water. White Tiger opened one of the parcels and found it contained smooth, rounded white buns.

"Ah!" exclaimed Mei, examining the contents of her own food bag. "Dumplings! Mei love dumplings."

"And these? What do I do with these? Never used them before."

White Tiger held up a pair of chopsticks he had found in the dragon's bag. He stabbed one into a bun and tried to eat it, unsuccessfully, like a lollipop. Mei giggled.

"No like that!" she laughed. "Watch!"

Mei proceeded to hold both chopsticks together in one hand, and using her small fingers was able to open and close them around a dumpling which she neatly picked up and popped into her mouth. White Tiger tried the same thing with his pair, and the bun he picked up fell, with one of the chopsticks, into his lap. Mei giggled again.

"I teach," she said. She put her own fingers around White Tiger's, showing him how to manipulate the chopsticks, thereby helping him carry a bun to his mouth.

"Now plactise!" she told him.

After a few tries, White Tiger felt he was getting the hang of eating with chopsticks. He even managed to use them to pick up lumps of sticky rice he found in one of the leaf parcels, but the peanuts defeated him, much to Mei's amusement, and he ended up using fingers instead. Just as he was about to put another peanut into his mouth he suddenly froze, his hand still holding the peanut in front of his open mouth. He glanced at Mei, for she, too, had gone very quiet. Quiet, and deathly pale, for there about twenty metres ahead of them the children saw a grey shape emerging from the side of a grey rock. At first it looked like a shadowy, shapeless blob that wobbled a bit like a large jelly as it separated itself from the rock. Then another and another of these blobs appeared from other rocks, until there were five shapeless lumps of quivering, grey jelly, and these started to move slowly in their direction. Mei gasped, and gripped White Tiger's arm tightly. As the grey blobs wobbled towards them the children saw that they gradually took the form of old bent figures with faces that were totally blank apart from narrow slits where their eyes should have been, and little round mouths.

"Mei scared," the girl said, trembling. She hid her face against White Tiger's shoulder. White Tiger realised these must be the *gui*, the restless ghosts of which the Blue Dragon had spoken. He, too, was scared, but tried to look brave for Mei's sake.

"Don't move," he whispered.

Carefully, he reached forward and pulled the dragon's bag towards him. The *gui* appeared to have gathered speed and were now walking on thin stick-like legs. Quickly, White Tiger unwrapped a dumpling and threw it at the feet of the nearest *gui*. The ghastly creature bent down, picked up the dumpling, and began munching it with its toothless mouth. White Tiger picked up four more dumplings and threw these at the other *gui*. By the time the last of the *gui* had started its dumpling, the

first one was finished and had begun to advance again menacingly and even more quickly towards the children. The food must have given it extra energy. White Tiger only had three dumplings left. He threw these at the *gui*, jumped up, grabbed Mei's hand and shouted "RUN!"

Together they ran as fast as they possibly could. When White Tiger was so breathless he felt he could go no further he stopped and turned round. To his horror the *gui* were still only twenty metres away and running as fast as the children had been.

"Faster, faster," he shouted to Mei, pulling her along.

"Can't," cried Mei. "Legs no go faster."

White Tiger glanced back and saw the hungry ghosts were gaining on them.

"At least if they get me you might escape," he cried out to the girl, thinking it was all *his* fault that they were there, anyway. "You go on ahead, and I'll stop and face them!"

"No!" sobbed Mei. "No leave you. Mei stay with White Tiger."

White Tiger stepped protectively between the silent ghosts and the Chinese girl and tried hard to look as fierce as a Roman legionary should, but his knees felt very shaky as the ghosts got nearer and nearer. He closed his eyes tightly and tried to imagine what it would feel like to have his body stolen from him. Would he become one of them? He was aware of Mei's arms encircling his waist from behind and that made him feel bolder.

Suddenly everything went dark. There was a great rush of wind and a terrific roar, just like he'd once heard from a lion at the Edinburgh Zoo.

"This is it!" he whispered as he felt Mei tighten her hold around his waist.

"Close one, children!" someone said.

White Tiger opened his eyes, just in time to see the *gui* turning back into formless lumps of jelly before they were sucked into a large rock only feet away from where he and Mei stood.

"Uh?" queried White Tiger looking up at the rock.

At first he was only aware of a splash of vivid colours on the top of the rock, but soon he made out the form of the weirdest of creatures that he had ever set eyes on. It had the head of a lion, which would have accounted for the roar, but the head was patchy blue and yellow and there was a horn in the middle of its forehead, like a unicorn's. Its purple, pink and red body was that of an enormous eagle-like bird with massive wings and large green-clawed feet. To complete the picture, it possessed a long, green, snaky tail which dangled from the rock down to the ground, and which must have been at least as long as a No. 62 bus. He wasn't a bit scared of it for, despite having the head of a lion, its face somehow looked very friendly. Mei had let her arms drop and now stood beside White Tiger.

"Um…" White Tiger began. "Who… I mean *what* are you?"

The creature looked down at its strange and colourful body and shrugged its wings.

"Not sure, really," it replied. "Looks like I'm a bit of this, a bit of that and a little bit of the other, don't you think?"

It glanced at its long green tail.

"They call me a Qilin, but to be frank I've no idea what a Qilin is. Or, for that matter, what it's supposed to do. But the

Jade Emperor's messenger told me to be ready to give you folks some help if needed. I asked the miserable old Blue Dragon where I could find you, but he wasn't terribly helpful. Kept on muttering about peaches, and would they be ripe yet, and complaining that the Red Phoenix didn't love him any more and that he almost felt like weeping he was so depressed. However, I assumed he was talking about the peaches in the garden of the Queen Mother of the West which only ripen once every sixteen thousand years. Must be thinking about making himself immortal! Anyway, pleased I found you before the *gui* got to you. Real nuisance, those restless ghosts! Can't think why the Jade Emperor puts up with them."

White Tiger was so glad to see Mei smiling again. He loved that smile of hers!

"Prease, Mr Qilin," she said. "We must find the garden of the Queen Mother of the West soon. White Tiger, he brave. Get led pearl and magical staff back for sad dragon. White Tiger think Monkey King who stole them go steal again. Steal magical peach."

"Um..." repeated White Tiger, looking rather distracted. "Er...did you just say once every sixteen thousand years? How long do the peaches stay ripe for?"

"Oh, a few days at the most," the Qilin replied cheerfully, jumping down from the rock to stand just in front of the children. "So," he said, looking at Mei, "you're the one they call Pretty Flower, eh? Must come from Hangzhou. Right?"

The girl nodded, whilst White Tiger stood there doing some quick mental arithmetic.

"If...er...just that if the peaches aren't ripe, we may...um...may have to wait sort of rather a long time," he observed.

"They *told* me he's bright," the Qilin said to Mei. "But if they're ripe, then hey presto! The Monkey King's sure to come a-thieving!"

"…every sixteen thousand years?"

White Tiger had been turning this over in his mind and he didn't fancy waiting that long.

"Correct!" exclaimed the Qilin. "You've a one in one-and-a-half million chance they'll be ripe tomorrow. That's pretty good! I'm an optimistic fellow, myself. Keep trying to persuade the Blue Dragon to be a little more optimistic, but he says he's feeling too sorry for himself to be optimistic just now."

"Do you know where this garden of the Queen Mother of the West is, by any chance?" asked White Tiger, feeling *far* from optimistic.

"Oh, it's about…er…let me see…I should say about…but this is an optimistic estimate…I would have thought somewhere in the region of…um…possibly…er…ten thousand *li*. Give or take, that is."

White Tiger felt very weak.

"Ten thousand *li*?" he repeated in a squeaky little voice.

"Mmm," confirmed the Qilin. "Good at mathematics?"

"He's the best in Peebles," Mei answered proudly, for White Tiger seemed to have lost his voice altogether.

"So if you can walk thirty *li* a day – that's optimistic, mind you, and there could be more *gui*, of course – but imagine if you *could* do thirty *li* a day, how long would it take to walk there?"

A funny high-pitched sound came out from White Tiger's mouth. He cleared his throat, and Mei put her arm round him to make him feel better.

"A year?" he suggested.

"So if during that time the peaches do get ripe, you know how long you'll have to wait!"

White Tiger nodded feebly.

"So?" questioned the Qilin.

White Tiger looked at Mei. Her face suddenly lit up.

"So White Tiger climb on back of Mr Qilin," she said confidently.

"Top of the class, Pretty Flower. I'll get you there in no time!"

White Tiger frowned.

"Why didn't he say that in the first place?" he muttered to himself.

The Qilin crouched down as the children climbed aboard his broad red back, and once again they soared up into the sky as the strange creature flapped its giant wings. White Tiger clutched on to the Qilin's feathers, praying he wouldn't pull them out accidentally, and Mei held on to White Tiger. The children thought the White Crane had flown fast, but in comparison with the Qilin the speed of the crane was nothing. They sped through the air so quickly that the ground below became a flashing blur beneath them.

CHAPTER 4: THE LADY SILKWORM

For the second time that day White Tiger and Mei found themselves flying high in the sky above hills, great plains, rivers and mountains. White Tiger thoroughly enjoyed the experience. It was something that Roman legionaries missed out on, normally. If only they had white cranes and qilins in Peebles, he thought. Then he and Andy could start up the airborne division of the Scottish Borders Roman Legion. He had already started to wonder about introducing changes to the legion. For example, where would Mei now fit in? That she should become a member of the legion when they got back home was without question. No doubt about it!

White Tiger turned to look at Mei. She was obviously loving the flight. He felt so happy to see *her* happy and he realised for the first time this was why he liked her so much. She just seemed to want to make others happy all the time.

"Why did the Qilin say you had to come from Hangzhou with a name like Pretty Flower?" he called back to the girl.

Mei looked a little embarrassed.

"In China say most beautiful women come from Hangzhou," she answered shyly.

"Oh!" said White Tiger, smiling. Looking at the girl behind him he could see how true that was.

After a few hours the Qilin slowed down, and White Tiger was able to make out a gentle landscape of rolling hills, with a pretty patchwork of colourful fields and orchards of fruit trees. They descended towards a small village and the Qilin landed in the courtyard of a large house at the edge of the village.

As soon as they had landed a plump, jolly man came running out of the house into the courtyard.

"Here they are, safe and sound!" he called to an equally jolly-looking woman standing in the doorway of the house.

"I found them just in time!" the Qilin said, as White Tiger and Mei slid down from his large back. "Just before the *gui* got to them. Anyway, they're here now, and if they can make the miserable old Blue Dragon less miserable, then we'll *all* be a lot happier!"

"So, Pretty Flower," the Jolly Man said to Mei, "it really is true what they say about you. That you look like your name!"

Mei gave the man a little bow.

"Preased to meet you, sir," she said.

"And this is White Tiger, the brave one?"

White Tiger bowed, wondering who had been going around telling people he was so brave.

"The Jade Emperor's messenger has told me all about you, White Tiger," said the Jolly Man.

It was as though he had read White Tiger's thoughts.

"Well," said the Qilin, "I must be going now, children, but just call me when you need me again."

"How do we do that?" asked White Tiger.

"Oh, I'll know if *you* know!" replied the Qilin.

White Tiger was puzzling over this, when Mei spoke to the creature.

"Wait, Mr Qilin!"

She reached up and kissed him on his large yellow cheek. White Tiger was sure there was a hint of red there as well after the girl had kissed him.

"*Xie xie*, Mr Qilin," Mei said, stroking the Qilin's large lion nose.

"My pleasure to be at your service!" the Qilin said. "Now step back, children. *Zai jian!*"

The Qilin spread his great wings and was gone in a flash.

"What does *zai jian* mean again?" White Tiger asked his friend. He had forgotten already.

"Mean goodbye," she replied.

"So," said the Jolly Man to the children. "Now you're here we'd better go and meet her, eh?"

"The Queen Mother of the West?" enquired White Tiger.

"Oh no," answered the man. "No one sees *her*. No, the Lady Silkworm."

White Tiger and Mei looked at each other.

"She's the only one who can help us make a net strong enough to hold the Monkey King. We'll use her magical gold silk. My wife can make the net with that, you see."

The children looked at the jolly wife. She waved at them and called out '*ni hao*' and they grinned and waved back at her.

"But how do we actually catch the Monkey King, sir?" asked White Tiger.

"Ah," replied the Jolly Man. "That's where Pretty Flower comes in. No point in trying to fight the Monkey King, White Tiger. He would *always* win, however brave you may be. Pretty Flower will have to charm him!"

"Me?" asked Mei, looking worried.

"You!" affirmed the Jolly Man, smiling. "With your dancing! That's why the Jade Emperor gave you that red dress to wear. His messenger said you came top in your dance class in Hangzhou."

Mei still looked a little anxious at the prospect of charming the bad monkey with her dancing.

"Come," said the Jolly Man, leading the children from the courtyard through a gateway into a grove of mulberry trees.

In the middle of this grove was a particularly large and ancient tree from which was hanging a most enormous, fat, worm-like thing, all wrapped up in a silk cocoon. Despite its huge size (it was at least as big as a horse) it had tiny little piggy eyes and a small round hole for a mouth from which dangled a thread of glistening golden silk.

"Lady Silkworm!" announced the Jolly Man. "First we must humour her, for she's been very grumpy of late. A bit like the Blue Dragon is at the moment. I know you'll find this hard to believe, children, but once upon a time this large lump of silk-producing blubber was a lively and beautiful young woman! Honest! You see, it's a rather sad story."

From the look on Mei's face White Tiger could tell that the girl was already feeling extremely sorry for Lady Silkworm.

"When she was a young woman her father disappeared, and she was so desperate to get him back that she unwisely said she would marry whosoever could find him. Their horse was standing within earshot of her when she said this and he immediately galloped off, found her father and returned him to the girl. The horse then asked her to marry him, but became very upset when she refused. She joked about this to her father who got angry with the horse for daring to want to marry his lovely daughter."

"Poor Lady Silkworm," said Mei. "Not good, girl marry horse."

"Poor horse too," continued the Jolly Man. "The father then shot the horse dead with an arrow. He skinned the dead horse and hung the skin out to dry. But the ghost of the horse's skin took its revenge on the beautiful young woman. It suddenly wrapped itself round the girl, turning her into what you see now. A giant silkworm. She's been hanging on that tree ever since, but the silk that comes from her mouth is the strongest material in the whole of heaven and earth. That's why we must use it to make the net for White Tiger to catch the Monkey King in. Wait here a moment. I'll talk to her."

The children looked on as the Jolly Man went up to Lady Silkworm and spoke to her. Her little piggy eyes blinked as he told her how useful her golden silk was and how important this made her. He added that if she were really, really good then perhaps one day the Jade Emperor would change her back into a beautiful young maiden.

The Jolly Man turned and winked at the children as they watched the Lady Silkworm blink a few times. Then her tiny mouth slowly opened wider and the golden thread hanging from it got longer and longer. The Jolly Man took a spindle from his pocket and wound the silk thread around this. As he wound the thread came out faster and faster, and soon the Jolly Man had to twiddle the spindle round to keep up with the silk. In a short while the spindle was covered with beautiful golden silk. Suddenly the flow of silk stopped. Lady Silkworm's little eyes closed and her mouth got smaller again. The Jolly Man took a diamond knife from his pocket and cut through the thread linking that small mouth to his spindle. Lady Silkworm was now completely still, just hanging there from the mulberry tree. Little Mei went right up to her and patted her very gently.

"*Xie xie*, poor Lady Silkworm," she said. "Mei ask Jade Emperor make you beautiful woman again. Marry handsome man, not horse."

Lady Silkworm opened her piggy eyes once more, and White Tiger was sure he could see little tears appearing in those eyes.

"*Zai jian!*" Mei whispered to her, and the children followed the Jolly Man back to the courtyard of his house and into the main building. His wife met them and took the spindle from her husband.

"She'll weave the strongest net you could possibly imagine," the Jolly Man said to White Tiger. "Not even the Monkey King will be able to break free from it. Now I'm sure you could both do with something to eat. You must be starving. And, do you know, my wife also happens to be the best cook in the world – and in heaven!"

The children were seated at a square table upon which dish after dish of the most wonderful food White Tiger had ever smelt or tasted kept appearing from the little kitchen adjacent to the living-room. He began to feel rather bloated and realised why the Jolly Man was so plump! He was also offered some peach juice which was simply delicious.

"Not magical peaches, I'm afraid," laughed the Jolly Man. "So you needn't worry about becoming immortal."

White Tiger had almost forgotten about the magical peaches. Would they have to wait sixteen thousand years? Once again the Jolly Man seemed to have read his mind:

"They'll be ripe tomorrow," he added. "So it's all working out pretty well, eh?"

"Where…?" began White Tiger.

"Oh, just up there on the hill behind our own orchard. That's the garden of the Queen Mother of the West. Nice sunny spot. With all the sun we've had today they should be just right to tempt that thieving monkey tomorrow."

White Tiger breathed a sigh of relief. Sixteen thousand years of food like that and White Tiger could imagine himself expanding to the size of the whole of Peebles!

"Tonight, children, you'll need a really good rest here, because you'll both have to be on top form for the challenge that faces you tomorrow. You see, so far nobody on earth or heaven has been able to contain the mischievous Monkey King. But the Jade Emperor has every confidence in you two. And he's sure to reward you if you're successful."

The only reward White Tiger could think of would be to get Mei safely back to her parents in Peebles. When he told this to the Jolly Man the fellow just smiled at him in a friendly way.

"I'm afraid the Jade Emperor can't do that. It's not how it works. But he will always be there to help you."

The Jolly Man sensed White Tiger's disappointment.

"Just let go of what you wish for, and things will work out," he said kindly.

Funny, thought White Tiger, that's just what Mei said to the Blue Dragon.

White Tiger and Mei were finally shown to a little room off the other side of the courtyard, and were delighted to see two beds with beautifully soft mattresses and silk bed covers. In no time at all the children were both fast asleep.

CHAPTER 5: MONKEY KING

White Tiger awoke feeling bright and refreshed, although he'd had the strangest dream ever. He dreamt he was in Peebles, and he was trying to get back to China because he thought he had left Mei behind there. He so desperately didn't want to lose his new friend and was more than relieved to see Mei lying on her mattress in her long, red silk dance dress, still asleep. He woke her up.

"Where are we?" the girl asked on opening her eyes. She looked alarmed.

"Seems we're still in China," said White Tiger. "Old China, anyway. But with a bit of luck we'll get back to Peebles today, Mei. Don't worry, I'll make sure you see your parents again very soon."

For some reason White Tiger was feeling extremely confident about everything.

"Miss parents very much," said Mei, looking rather sad.

"Aye," said White Tiger. "Me too. And Andy. He's the only Roman legionary left in our camp until I return. And Mei, when we're back in Peebles we'll have to think of a Roman legionary name for you."

"Girl soldier?" she asked, pulling a bit of a face. "No like girl soldier."

"We could call you Mea Maxima," White Tiger suggested eagerly.

"No like," Mei said. "Prefer Hua-Mei."

"Think I do as well," agreed White Tiger. "You could still come to our camp as Mei," he added. "Could be a Chinese cook, or something. Maybe we could start up a Romano-Chinese takeaway!"

"Prefer Chinese princess," said Mei, frowning.

"Great!" exclaimed White Tiger. "You could be our Romano-Chinese princess. Princess Hua-Mei! Sounds good. A deal then, for when get back, eh?"

White Tiger offered his hand and they shook on it. White Tiger thought it was really cool that they now had a Chinese princess in their legion. He couldn't wait to get back to Peebles and inform Andius Minimus.

It was at this point in time that the Jolly Man came into their room.

"Sleep well, children?" he asked.

Together they nodded.

"Up for it then, both of you? Capturing the mischievous Monkey King?"

They nodded again.

"And you, Pretty Flower. Have you a dance ready to charm the wicked thief?"

"Do Monkey King Dance," she replied, grinning.

"And White Tiger? Will you be quick enough to slip this net over the Monkey King once Pretty Flower has him charmed?"

The Jolly Man handed White Tiger the rolled up net of golden silk. White Tiger unfurled it. It was very large, and the silk was very fine. Stretched out it was almost invisible, but pull at it as he might, he could not tear it.

"Practise on me! Like this – wham!" the Jolly Man said, sitting on a stool with his back to White Tiger and demonstrating how the boy should whisk the net over his body. White Tiger had a few shots at slipping the net over the Jolly Man. It made Mei laugh, but he was amazingly quick and the Jolly Man was genuinely impressed.

"I've a feeling this is going to go well today and Monkey King will at long last get what he deserves. Of course, you have one big advantage that no one else could have over the monkey... you're children! He'll never suspect that you're up to something. Another reason why the Jade Emperor chose you, you see! Ready?"

"*Dui*," Mei and White Tiger said together.

"Off we go then!"

The Jolly Man took them to the foot of the hill, and pointed to the path leading up to the garden of the Queen Mother of the West.

"I can't go any further myself," said the Jolly Man. "If the Monkey King were to see me he'd smell a rat, so to speak! From now on you're on your own."

The children went on alone up the narrow path to the magical peach garden at the top. It was very beautiful, and the peaches were so ripe that White Tiger could even smell their scent in the warm air. How lucky they were, he thought. Only once every sixteen thousand years! In the centre of the garden was a small clearing, and here the children found a log to sit on and wait for the Monkey King. White Tiger tried to imagine his friend dancing.

"Mei, how will you be able to dance without music?" White Tiger asked.

It had suddenly occurred to him that they didn't have a CD player!

"No music, no plobrem!" the girl answered.

"No problem!" White Tiger corrected, smiling.

"No pro...blem!" she repeated, and laughed. "Music in head."

Mei tapped the side of her head and grinned at White Tiger.

Clever girl, thought White Tiger, feeling very proud to be her friend.

It was whilst he was thinking this that the Monkey King suddenly materialised. It was quite extraordinary. He seemed to appear from nowhere, for all of a sudden there he was, standing right in front of the children, holding a long golden staff in one hand and a soft, ripe, pink peach in the other. All they had noticed was a sort of rushing sound and a flash of yellow and brown way up in the clouds. White Tiger assumed the monkey had grabbed a peach on his way down to the ground.

The Monkey King was dressed in a fine yellow trouser suit, with a pearl-studded golden crown on his head, and his long, curly tail stuck out at the back.

"So!" he said imperiously. "What are you children doing in *my* peach garden?"

The children stood up.

"It's not..." began White Tiger, but he stopped when he felt a familiar pinch on his arm. He knew that meant let Mei do the talking, so he shut up!

Mei stepped forward.

"Oh, great Mr Monkey King," she said, bowing very low. "We come to entertain his majesty. Give enjoyment."

"Oh you have, have you?" asked the Monkey King. "And what makes you think I want to be entertained, eh? Do you really think a great king who is about to become immortal (he looked at the peach in his hand) is at all interested in the antics of two children?"

"Hua-Mei best Chinese dancer in class in Hangzhou," Mei persisted.

"*And* in Peebles!" added White Tiger eagerly.

"Peebles?" queried the Monkey King. "Now *that* sounds interesting. Don't have a dancer from Peebles in my court. In fact, don't know of any other immortal who has a dancer from Peebles. I might just rest a little on that log there, Pretty Flower, and watch your dance whilst I eat my peach."

"Oh, Mr Monkey King, prease no eat peach same time. May get indigestion if eat and watch together. Monkey King bad tummy make Hua-Mei velly sad."

Mei put on such a convincingly sad expression that the Monkey King put the peach aside as he sat on the log. He also flung the magical golden staff, stolen from the Blue Dragon, to the ground.

"Won't need that, will I? Not with two children, ha-ha!" he joked and laughed. White Tiger and Mei laughed along with him.

"Hua-Mei want make Monkey King happy," Mei said, smiling very prettily at the monkey.

"Feel happy already just to look at you, Pretty Flower," announced the monkey. "Not sure about him, though," he added, scowling at White Tiger.

"No, no," said White Tiger. "In my country of Peebles a mortal must always stand behind an immortal when there's any

...er...dancing going on. Yes, he has to stand there, behind the immortal, and...er...um...make sure that...er...nobody disturbs him. Immortals don't like to be disturbed if they're watching dancing. That is, Chinese dancing. And that's a fact!"

The Monkey King eyed White Tiger suspiciously. White Tiger glanced nervously at Mei.

"White Tiger say true," she lied, walking gracefully up to the seated Monkey King and lifting her arms to show him the long, slender, silken sleeves of her red dance dress. "White Tiger guard Monkey King so majesty can relax."

Mei started to dance, and the Monkey King couldn't take his eyes off her. Quietly, White Tiger slipped round to the back of the monkey, taking care not to tread on his long tail. He took the net of golden silk from his pocket and began unravelling it as Mei continued her dance. When the net was ready White Tiger looked up at the girl, thinking her dancing was simply beautiful. He had never seen anything so graceful in all his life. He loved the way she turned and twisted and created circles and spirals in the air with her trailing sleeves. In fact, he was beginning to feel entranced by the beauty of the dance himself when he noticed that the Monkey King had gone very still indeed. White Tiger could tell from the look Mei gave him as she twirled herself round once more that now was the time! Unobserved by the captivated monkey, White Tiger raised the golden silk net high in the air, and WHAM! In a flash it was right down over the Monkey King. Immediately the monkey began shouting and kicking and punching, but all to no avail. He was totally trapped in the strong net. Mei ran forwards and picked up the magical staff, and White Tiger grabbed the peach of immortality from the log beside the struggling Monkey King.

"Why, you thieving little blighters!" exclaimed the monkey. "You wait till I get out of this net. I'll teach you a thing or two, I will. Should never trust a woman, eh? Just a common thief!"

"And hark who's talking!" protested White Tiger. "Don't you dare call Hua-Mei a thief again, you miserable robber. That staff she's holding belongs to the Blue Dragon. It's not yours at all. This garden belongs to the Queen Mother of the West, not you, and that magical peach, that's hers as well. And there's another thing we mean to get back from you! The Blue Dragon's red pearl. Where is it? We know you stole it."

White Tiger was angry with the Monkey King for calling Mei a thief. He didn't like that at all.

"Don't know anything about a red pearl!" the Monkey King said sullenly, trying in vain to tear the net of silk.

"Oh yes you do!" said White Tiger.

"Oh no I don't!" protested the monkey.

"Oh yes you..." White Tiger was going to continue, but stopped when he realised it wasn't getting them anywhere.

"If you don't tell us where it is we'll hand you over to the black tortoise."

White Tiger could think of nothing more frightening on the spur of the moment.

"Not scared of *him*," the Monkey King said.

"Will be if we give the tortoise the dragon's staff."

"You wouldn't do that – would you?"

The Monkey King had stopped struggling, and began to look worried.

"Who says I wouldn't?" said White Tiger, still very cross that his friend had been maligned.

The Monkey King appeared to be mulling things over in his mind.

"If..." he began, "if I tell you, will you give me back my peach?"

"Not your peach!" replied White Tiger. "But..."

White Tiger held the peach in front of the mischievous monkey's nose and watched his nostrils begin to twitch.

"If we get the red pearl back for the dragon, then maybe if he's in a *really* good mood he'll let you have one bite. How about it?"

"Pah!" exclaimed an infuriated Monkey King. He looked at White Tiger, then at Mei and then back at White Tiger.

"Tai Shan!" he said. "That's where it is. Though, mind you, I made a lot more use of it than that miserable old dragon did. Made loads of money. If you come in with *me* then I'll give you some."

"Tai Shan?" White Tiger asked Mei, ignoring the monkey's attempt to bribe them. "Isn't it that the holy mountain, Mei? Near the Blue Dragon's cave in Shan...pong?"

"Shandong!" Mei laughed. "*Dui!*"

"Oh dear! That means we have to go all the way back again. What did the Qilin say to do if...?"

There was a flash of bright colours, a loud beating of huge wings, and there he was – the Qilin – right in the middle of the clearing! He bowed to White Tiger and Mei.

"How's that for service?" he asked.

"Pretty good!" replied White Tiger, impressed.

"Ah!" said the Qilin looking down at the wretched monkey. "You have him! Somehow I knew you'd be successful."

"Aye," said White Tiger. "But he's gone and hidden the dragon's red pearl on Tai Shan. That's a long way off. We just wondered whether…"

"No problem. Jump on, kids. You know the drill by now!"

"*Xie xie,*" said Mei. "Mr Qilin so kind."

So the children climbed onto the Qilin's back once again, White Tiger in front, and Mei behind him. The Qilin unceremoniously picked up the Monkey King, much to the simian's annoyance, with one of his great claws, and took off into the air.

"We're first class and he's in the luggage hold," White Tiger joked, and Mei laughed. As before, she looked really happy to be flying at such an incredible speed on the back of the strange animal. She had an arm around White Tiger's waist whilst White Tiger gripped the Qilin's strong feathers. He had managed to shrink the magical golden staff down to the size of a pencil and it was safely tucked away in his pocket.

"Mr Qilin!" White Tiger shouted. "We didn't say thank you to the Jolly Man for all his help. Will you thank him for us, please?"

"Him?" laughed the Qilin. "But he's anywhere and everywhere. You can thank him any time you wish."

White Tiger, puzzled, just shrugged his shoulders.

It was a long flight again, right across China, even at the speed of a Qilin, but the children enjoyed every minute of it. Every time White Tiger turned to look at Mei she was smiling. Somehow her smiles always had the power to make him feel warm and happy inside.

At one point in the flight they slowed down a little. The Qilin told White Tiger to look at the ground below. There the boy saw an enormous wall stretching away in the distance to the north and to the south, as it snaked over hills and mountains and across valleys and deserts. Excitedly, White Tiger turned round to Mei to ask her about it.

"Great Wall of China!" she explained. "First Emperor build more than two thousand years ago. Make bigger later. Keep out enemy. Mongol enemy."

"Was he the Jade Emperor?"

"No," laughed Mei. "First Emperor on *earth*. Jade Emperor *heaven*."

White Tiger was very confused about earth emperors and heaven emperors, and who did what and when! A while later he spotted Tai Shan, the holy mountain, from a long way off. As they approached it he was able to make out several beautiful buildings on the summit, all with curvy Chinese roofs.

"Look, Mei," he said to his friend. "There are buildings on the top of the mountain."

"*Dui*," said Mei. "Temple. Many people climb mountain see temple. *Baba* say one day he take me. Many steps to top, but now cable-car make easy."

White Tiger looked carefully at the mountain.

"I see the steps, Mei, but no cable car!" he called back to the girl. He was going to say 'it hasn't been built…' but wasn't sure whether to say 'now' or 'then'. After all, the cable-car wasn't there 'now', but that's because they saw the mountain 'then', so to speak. He was beginning to feel *very* muddled about time. If it was 'then' back in Peebles where were his parents? Were they in caves, as Mrs Kerr had suggested might be the case? He didn't fancy returning to Peebles to live in a cave! Perhaps, he thought, the *real* Romans would be there, in which case he and Andius Minimus should be okay.

The Qilin came in to land in front of a large temple building. He dropped the netted Monkey King just before touching ground. The monkey made an awful fuss, howling and screaming and saying that this was no way to treat royalty.

"Some royalty," said White Tiger, as he helped the monkey to his feet. "Now, where's the Blue Dragon's red pearl?"

The Monkey King rubbed his bruised bottom.

"Don't see why I should tell you," he protested petulantly.

White Tiger sighed.

"No red pearl, no peach," he said, removing the peach from his pocket and holding it in front of the monkey's twitching nose again. The Monkey King's greedy eyes lit up at the sight of the magical fruit.

"Peach first, then pearl!" he demanded, folding his arms across his chest.

"Don't trust a monkey!" warned the Qilin who had been standing cleaning his red feathers with his large lion tongue.

"You keep out of this, you crazy mixed-up animal," the monkey said unkindly.

White Tiger could see that the Qilin rather took the monkey's remark to heart. The strange animal looked at his claws and his long snake tail. He opened his wings out again and stared at them. Just when White Tiger thought the Qilin was about to burst into tears little Mei ran up to the creature, put her arms around his neck and kissed his large, furry yellow cheek again.

"We love you velly much Mr Qilin," she said. "Mr Qilin velly kind. *Xie xie!*"

"Do you both really love me? I mean, even *I* don't know what or who I am! Just a crazy, mixed-up animal, I suppose."

"No you're not," said Mei, hugging the Qilin. "Mr Qilin most wonderful animal in world."

"Oh!" exclaimed the Qilin.

A smile appeared on the Qilin's huge lion mouth.

"Aye. And that includes Peebles," added White Tiger with sincerity. "When we get back to Peebles we'll tell them all about the wonderful Mr Qilin in China."

"Do you know…?" began the Qilin.

The children looked at him.

"Do you know that there's a lady Qilin somewhere down south? White Crane told me once. I didn't think she'd be interested in me, but…"

The Qilin looked bashfully at Mei.

"What does Pretty Flower think?" he asked.

"She think Mr Qilin must go to lady Qilin!" replied Mei, smiling.

"You should find the Blue Dragon's cave quite easily by yourselves, now," the Qilin assured the children. "You can see his little mountain ahead of you from the foot of the steps."

"Aye, I saw those steps," said White Tiger.

"So, perhaps, if you don't mind, you might excuse me to…er…um…"

Mei laughed.

"Go, Mr Qilin! Go see lady Qilin now!" she said.

"*Zai jian* then!" the Qilin said. "If you ever need me in Peebles, you know what to do. Although I do have a slight problem there, because I have no idea where Peebles is."

White Tiger laughed.

"I don't think you're the only one, Mr Qilin!"

The children both bid the kind Qilin farewell, and watched as he flew off to the south.

"Just one bite, then!"

White Tiger turned round. He had almost forgotten about the Monkey King.

"What?" he crossly asked the grovelling simian.

"One bite. Then I show you where the red pearl is hidden. Otherwise we can all sit and wait, and I can wait a few hundred years if needs be. Just sitting here."

White Tiger looked at Mei. She was beginning to appear upset and he so wanted to get her back to her parents. He felt he had to do something, so he picked up a piece of sharp flint stone from the ground and cut a small wedge from the flesh of the peach. It smelt heavenly and White Tiger noticed the Monkey King's twitching nostrils go into overdrive as he held up the piece of peach. The monkey closed his eyes and opened his mouth. White Tiger didn't like the look of his sharp teeth. He still had his chopsticks in his pocket, so he took these out and asked Mei to use them to poke the peach slice into the monkey's mouth. She accomplished this with her usual grace and skill and the children watched as the Monkey King savoured the peach. A look of ecstasy appeared on the monkey's ugly face. It went through a series of amazing contortions of pleasure which caused Mei to lift her hand to her mouth and giggle.

"Funny monkey!" she whispered to White Tiger.

Finally the monkey swallowed the mouthful of peach with one great gluttonous gulp. He stared at White Tiger.

"More!" he commanded, like a king ordering one of his subjects.

"Oh, no way, you fiendish monkey," said White Tiger. "The red pearl first! And *I* can wait a thousand years, if necessary. The trouble is the peach can't wait. It'll be all horrible and smelly in a day or two!"

White Tiger was a quick learner! He was determined to outwit the wily Monkey King at his own game.

"Pah!" exclaimed the exasperated monkey. "It's behind me! In that temple, under the altar with the golden statue."

"Keep an eye on him," White Tiger called to Mei as he entered the temple to retrieve the dragon's pearl. And there, in the temple, he got the shock of his life!

Seated on the altar was the golden statue of a happy man with a large rounded belly, but in front of White Tiger's very eyes the statue changed into a real person. And *that* person was none other than the Jolly Man who lived beside the garden of the Queen Mother of the West...the man whose wife had made the net of golden silk for them and who had fed them and put them up for the night. He rushed back to the entrance of the temple and called out to Mei.

"Mei! Come quick. In here!"

Mei came running.

"Oh!" she exclaimed. "Lord Buddha!"

Mei knelt in front of the Jolly Man, put her hands together and bowed right down to the ground three times. White Tiger copied her, thinking it the right thing to do. He remembered she

had told him her *Kung-Kung* was a Buddhist, and at school Mrs Kerr had said something about Buddhists when they were doing religion, but he couldn't believe they were now kneeling in front of the Lord Buddha himself.

"Lord Buddha, prease, so solly…" began Mei.

"Quiet, my Pretty Flower," the Lord Buddha interrupted kindly. "You and White Tiger have excelled yourselves. You've fulfilled your destiny, and I'm so very pleased with you."

White Tiger felt guilty for having given the Monkey King a slice of the peach of immortality, and he wondered whether he'd get into trouble for this.

"But Lord Buddha," he said weakly, "I did a bad thing. I gave in to the Monkey King because I was so desperate to find the red pearl so that I can get Mei back to Peebles to be with her parents again."

"That, brave White Tiger, was part of your destiny too," said Lord Buddha. "The red pearl is here, underneath the altar upon which I'm sitting. Take it, White Tiger. Take it and the magical staff in your pocket, and go with Pretty Flower to the Blue Dragon. He's expecting you. As for the Monkey King, he has chosen his own path and still has many lessons to learn. It was predictable. Don't worry. He won't become immortal from taking just one bite of the peach. If he desires immortality he has to pass another test."

White Tiger glanced back through the doorway of the temple.

"Lord Buddha he…he's…g-g-gone!" he stuttered, looking in horror at the empty courtyard outside. "The Monkey King's gone! Oh, Lord Buddha!"

Lord Buddha smiled. In fact, he hadn't *stopped* smiling at the children. He slowly shook his large head and held out his hand, opening it for White Tiger to see. White Tiger gasped, for there, squirming about, was a tiny version of the Monkey King, complete with yellow suit and a golden crown. He even held a staff in his small hand. White Tiger and Mei looked at each other, incredulous.

"Don't worry, it's not the magical one; you've still got that. But he'll need something where he's going. Our Monkey King still has much to learn," Lord Buddha said, looking down benignly at the irate little figure in his hand. "Maybe one day he *will* learn, and I shall try to help him. Meanwhile, if he wants immortality he's going to have to jump out of my hand. He, who can leap thousands of *li* with one somersault, might think that an easy task, but we'll see. Forget the Monkey King now, children. Leave him in my hands, so to speak! That's where *his* destiny lies. You've got far more important things to do. First, White Tiger, take the red pearl and the magical staff to the Blue Dragon. Everyone will be delighted if you and Pretty Flower can cheer him up."

Bowing low, White Tiger reached forward under the stone altar. His fingers touched something smooth and round. Slowly and cautiously he pulled out a large red globe, about the size of a football. It was curiously light to hold, and shone with a faint pink glow. Terrified that he might drop it, he carefully handed it to his friend. It looked huge in her small hands.

"Here, Mei," he said. "I think it'll be safer with you."

"Be quick, children," said Lord Buddha. "The Blue Dragon's cave is getting very full of water. That carpet over there will get you to the bottom of Tai Shan, then just follow the path to the dragon's little mountain. And do watch out for the black tortoise. You may use the magical staff, White Tiger, if he annoys you."

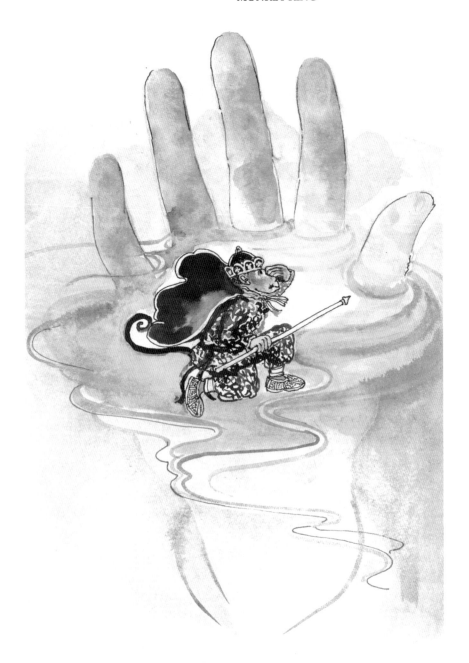

CHAPTER 6:
THE GREY TORTOISE AND THE BLACK TORTOISE

The children bowed respectfully, and when they were upright again they saw only a motionless golden Buddha statue on the altar. They left the temple using the patterned carpet the Lord Buddha had pointed out. They stood together on the carpet and in an instant they were at the foot of Tai Shan, looking towards the small conical mountain where the Blue Dragon had his cave. There was no cloud at all over the top of the mountain and, remembering what the White Crane had said, White Tiger took this to be a very bad sign indeed.

"We must hurry," he said to Mei as they started along the path towards the dragon's mountain. They went as quickly as they could, but Mei couldn't run whilst holding the precious red pearl in both hands. Soon they reached a fast-flowing stream, and the path coursed alongside this towards the mountain.

Suddenly Mei, who was in front, halted. White Tiger stopped too, for there, just a few metres ahead, was a large humpy grey rock that was definitely moving towards them. The rock stopped just in front of Mei who trembled so much that White Tiger was afraid she might drop the red pearl. He stepped protectively in front of the girl and took the magical staff from his pocket. Then a head popped out from the rock, and Mei laughed. The rock was only a giant tortoise.

"Some tortoise!" said White Tiger, as the creature looked from Mei to White Tiger, and back at Mei.

"*Ni hao!*" the tortoise said. "Yes, I am *some* tortoise, but I'm not black, so I'm all right. I'm not into fighting, like my cousin. They usually call me the Grey Tortoise, but it doesn't make any odds really. Call me what you like, so long as it's not 'Black Tortoise'."

The Grey Tortoise was very slow. White Tiger was afraid it might delay them. Nevertheless, he didn't want to appear rude. In a ponderous sort of a way the tortoise also looked friendly, and he and Mei needed friends in this place.

"*Ni hao!* But why legs so short, Mr Grey Tortoise?" Mei asked.

She was referring to its stumpy little legs. Even for a tortoise they were very short.

"Much longer, they were, once upon a time. But they got cut off, see."

"Poor Mr Grey Tortoise," said Mei, frowning. "Why legs cut off?"

"Oh, it's a long story," replied the Grey Tortoise, sadly. "It's a *very* long story. Do you have a very long time to hear it?"

White Tiger looked anxiously at Mei. They didn't have a very long time, but he could tell the Grey Tortoise was extremely keen to tell them the tale about his legs getting cut off.

"I don't think…" he began.

"Hear Grey Tortoise story about cut-off legs," Mei interrupted, winking at White Tiger. "But if legs now short maybe story also short."

The Grey Tortoise looked very thoughtful.

"Well…" he began very slowly. "Long story, just like my life, but in short, so to speak, my short legs became short because Nu

Wa cut them off to use as props for heaven when that crazy dragon, Gong-Gong, went berserk and did all that damage knocking down the supports of heaven."

"Nu Wa? The one who made the first people out of mud?"

White Tiger remembered what the Blue Dragon had told him.

"Her!" affirmed the Grey Tortoise.

"She used your legs to do that? Couldn't she have used anything else?" queried White Tiger.

"Apparently not," replied the Grey Tortoise, turning its wrinkled head to get a better view of its stumpy little legs. It was beginning to look very sorry for itself. "But the Jade Emperor, he was pleased with my self-sacrifice, and said I can live on for ever and ever as a result. Mind you…"

The Grey Tortoise paused.

"Mind you," he repeated, "I haven't really decided yet whether that's a good or a bad thing – to live forever. What do you children think? I've been wondering about it for thousands of years ever since my legs were cut off."

White Tiger was lost for words, but Mei wasn't.

"Oh, Mr Grey Tortoise," she said. "So happy you alive. If no carry magic red pearl for Brue Dragon would do Grey Tortoise dance for you."

"Really?"

The Grey Tortoise suddenly no longer looked sad.

"*Dui*," said the girl. "When Hua-Mei back in Peebles she do Grey Tortoise dance and tell everyone in Peebles what nice tortoise is Mr Grey Tortoise."

Not only did the Grey Tortoise no longer appear sad, he actually looked quite happy.

"So, Pretty Flower, that red pearl you're holding – is there a long story about that too?" he asked slowly. "I'd love to hear it if there is one."

Oh dear, thought White Tiger. As briefly as possible they told the Grey Tortoise how the Monkey King had tricked the Blue Dragon and stolen his red pearl and magical staff and how Mei had charmed the Monkey King with her dancing, and how he had netted the monkey and brought him back to Tai Shan where they had met Lord Buddha.

"If you meet my cousin, the Black Tortoise, be sure you knock him back to Dongbei in the north with that magical staff," said the Grey Tortoise. "It wouldn't do to send him down south. Wouldn't do at all! See, he comes from the north and he shouldn't really be down this way. You'll be doing everyone a favour if you send him flying off to the right place. Dongbei, that is. But take care. He's good at fighting. Meanwhile I'll just stop here for a few hundred years and sit and imagine Pretty Flower doing the Grey Tortoise dance. You know, I think I'll actually enjoy that. Being alive, and imagining her doing her dance. I do like her red dress."

"The Jade Emperor gave it to her. Especially to charm the Monkey King."

Slowly the Grey Tortoise's head shrank back within its ancient shell. White Tiger heard some muffled words like 'charming' and 'Peebles' and 'Grey Tortoise dance' coming out from the opening in the shell.

"*Zai Jian!*" the children called out together into the old grey shell.

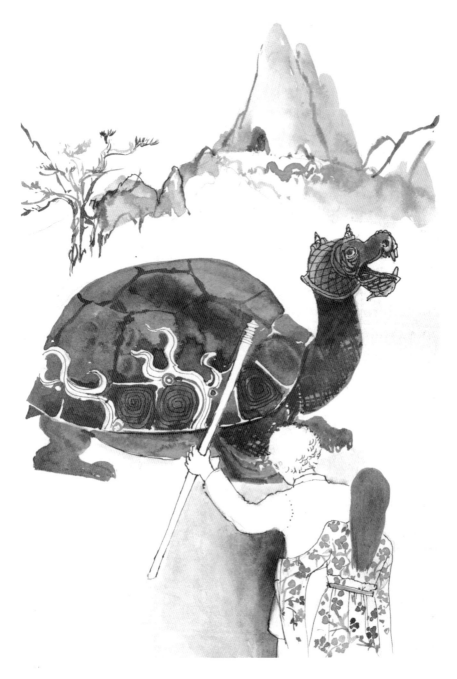

"...red pearl...Monkey King...Blue Dragon...Peebles..."
muttered the tortoise to itself.

Mei giggled, and White Tiger couldn't help thinking once
more how the girl made everyone, including himself, feel so
happy. Everyone, that is, apart from the Monkey King. But there
again, even *he* enjoyed her Monkey King dance.

The children left the Grey Tortoise in the middle of the path
and continued on towards the cloudless, small mountain.

"At last," White Tiger said to Mei when the path left the
stream and they began to ascend towards the Blue Dragon's
cave. "Oh dear," he added a moment later, when a huge black
rock leapt out on to the path just ahead of them!

Apart from having a shell, the Black Tortoise was nothing like
its gentle cousin, the Grey Tortoise. It was far larger, it had long,
strong legs and had a shiny helmet on its ugly head. It looked
positively evil!

White Tiger ran in front of Mei, who was terrified, and pulled
out the magical staff. Immediately it turned into a thick rod of
gold, at least three metres long. It should have been far too
heavy for a boy of ten to hold, but somehow it seemed
weightless in White Tiger's hands. Not only that. *It* appeared to
control White Tiger rather than the other way around.

"I've heard all about you!" warned White Tiger. "You
shouldn't be here, anyway."

"Who told you that?" asked the Black Tortoise. "That pathetic
little cousin of mine?"

White Tiger didn't like the shifty look on the Black Tortoise's
face. He tensed his muscles as he gripped the golden staff even
more tightly.

"One step closer and I'll send you packing!" he told the Black Tortoise.

"Oh, surely you wouldn't hurt an unarmed tortoise, would you?"

There was a wickedness in the eyes of the Black Tortoise. White Tiger caught sight of a glint of cold steel from a collection of swords peeping out from the edge of the creature's coal-black shell. Unarmed indeed! Suddenly the Black Tortoise flicked out a large sword and ran at White Tiger. It had arms and legs just like a man's! The magical staff simply took over for White Tiger. It lifted his arms in the air, and also caused his own legs to rush forwards. The Black Tortoise was completely taken by surprise. Before it had time to raise its sword against White Tiger, the boy had whacked it so hard across the side of its shell that it shot right up into the air. It continued to go higher and higher and higher into the sky. Thankfully it had gone off in a northerly direction. Perhaps the magical staff had thought about that when it took control of White Tiger's arms.

"Good riddance!" exclaimed White Tiger as he watched the black dot of the receding Black Tortoise disappear into a cloud.

"Good what?" asked Mei who couldn't think of anything good about the Black Tortoise.

"Oh, just a saying in Peebles," he replied. "Good riddance to bad rubbish."

"Like Confucius saying?" questioned the girl.

"Con...who?"

White Tiger looked puzzled.

"Wise man. Long ago in China. Called Confucius. My *Kung-Kung* teach me," said Mei. "Many sayings. Wise sayings. Like 'beauty in everything, not everyone sees it'."

"Everything?" queried White Tiger. "Even the Monkey King and the Black Tortoise?"

"*Dui!*" replied Mei, looking quite serious. "Bad people maybe one day beauty in them get stronger and turn good. That's why Lord Buddha teach bad monkey lesson."

"Hmm!" exclaimed White Tiger. He wasn't convinced, but he wanted to believe her.

"Tell you what, Mei. When you become our Romano-Chinese princess you could teach Andy and me a few things about Lord Buddha...and about Confuse-us."

"Confucius!" giggled Mei.

"Aye, him. You could tell us more about these things. Okay?"

"*Xing!*" agreed Mei. "Make Mei velly happy!"

"And...well, would you, um...er...would you dance for us? Chinese dancing, like the Grey Tortoise dance, or something?"

"*Dui,*" the girl said. "Give Mei much preasure!"

"Pleasure. L...L...L...!" laughed White Tiger.

"Pleasure. L...L...L...!" repeated Mei.

The children had been walking up to the ledge outside the dragon's cave whilst they talked. On approaching this they were somewhat surprised to see a little waterfall tipping over the edge.

"Oh no!" exclaimed White Tiger. "What's the betting he hasn't stopped crying since we left him yesterday. Come on!"

They scrambled up onto the ledge, and sure enough the whole area had turned into a little lake.

"Oh dear!" muttered White Tiger as they waded into the cave up to their knees in water. There was a very loud bubbling sound coming from the back of the cave. The Blue Dragon's large nostrils were now half-submerged and huge bubbles were being blown into the water each time the dragon breathed out. Only the tops of his eyes showed and his droopy eyelids were closed over these. Inside the cave the water level was up to the children's waists. White Tiger held Mei's hand, for he didn't want any more drowning episodes to happen to her.

"Dear Mr Brue Dragon," said Mei reaching up to talk softly into one of the dragon's droopy ears. "All right now. White Tiger get red pearl and magical staff. See!"

One great eyelid flicked open, and the Blue Dragon peered at the girl.

"Okay for dragon boat-race," she added. "Now Led Phoenix come back to lovely Brue Dragon."

Mei nearly fell over when the Blue Dragon suddenly lifted his vast head out of the water, and White Tiger had to catch hold of her. The dragon blinked a few times at the children.

"Oh, my pearl, my pearl, Pretty Flower. You have my pearl!"

"Er…one little problem, Mr Blue Dragon," said White Tiger, looking around at all the water in the cave. "Where can Hua-Mei put it? There's so much water! We have the magical staff, too. See!"

White Tiger took the staff from his under-water pocket, and it immediately turned into a long rod of gold again.

"Oh, wonderful! How can I thank you both?"

"We'll come to that in a moment. Meanwhile where can we...?"

White Tiger suddenly stopped when the Blue Dragon raised more of his body above the water. For the first time he got an idea of the true size of the beast. He was simply enormous! His body alone was larger than a double-decker bus. Just by lifting most of his bulk out of the water, the water-level went down considerably, and White Tiger could now see the ground along the side of the cave.

"Wow!" he exclaimed, looking up at the magnificent creature.

The dragon gently lifted an enormous clawed foot and carefully took the red pearl and the golden staff from the children. He held the magical objects and stared at them for a while.

"Nothing I can do could ever repay you children for what you've done," he said. "Nothing! You've given me back a *reason* to be a blue dragon. I can help the farmers now!"

The Blue Dragon placed the red pearl and golden staff on the ground at the edge of the cave. The pearl glowed a luminous pink in the dim light and the dragon began to play with it, rolling it back and forth. Just like a kitten playing with a ball of wool, thought White Tiger.

"There is something you *could* do for us. Well, we hope you could do it for us," White Tiger said.

"Yes?" queried the distracted dragon, still playing with his red pearl.

"You could tell us how to get back to Peebles. Hua-Mei is missing her parents terribly."

"Peebles?" the dragon muttered, picking up the golden rod and gently tapping the red pearl with it. "Peebles? Where's Peebles?"

"It's where we live. In the Scottish Borders!"

"The Scottish Borders? Where's that?"

The Blue Dragon still didn't seem to be paying him any proper attention, and White Tiger felt himself getting very cross.

"Look, Mr Dragon," he began to say, "we've been all the way to…"

He was interrupted by a gentle pinch on his arm. He knew he should leave the talking to Mei once again.

"Oh, noble Mr Brue Dragon, Led Phoenix so preased when she hear how you help get boy and girl back to Peebles. She love dragon who help boy and girl. Especially boy and girl from Peebles."

The dragon stopped playing with the red pearl and turned his huge head to look at her. His plate-like eyes went all dreamy-looking.

"Will she now?" he asked.

"Mmm," affirmed Mei. "Led Phoenix velly ploud of helpful Brue Dragon."

"Well, you could ask the Moon Rabbit," suggested the Blue Dragon.

"The *what*?" exclaimed White Tiger angrily.

"Shhh!" went Mei, holding a finger to her mouth for White Tiger.

"Moon Rabbit," repeated the Blue Dragon. "Knows everything, does the jade rabbit on the moon. He's sure to know how you could get back to Peebles."

"How get there? Moon?" asked Mei gently.

"Blinking space shuttle!" an annoyed White Tiger muttered under his breath.

"Shhh!"

Mei tried to calm him down again.

"Easy-peasy!" replied the Blue Dragon. He still had that 'I'm thinking about Red Phoenix' look in his eyes. "White Crane! He'll take you. If you ask him very nicely, that is."

This was too much for White Tiger.

"White Crane? How on earth can a flipping bird fly to the moon?"

"Flaps his wings, I suppose," murmured Blue Dragon. The far-away look in his eyes was getting more and more far-away. "Look, I must see my belovéd Red Phoenix soon. Do you think that I should fly down to see her next week, Pretty Flower?"

"Think should go," replied Mei.

"Or tomorrow perhaps?" continued the Blue Dragon. "I think I'll fly south tomorrow. No, how about later today, or…?"

The dragon shifted his vast bulk.

"Why…er…um…?"

"Yes?" the children said together.

"…don't I…um…er…?"

"Yes?" repeated the children.

"…well…go…NOW?"

The Blue Dragon almost trod on White Tiger with his large foot as he raised himself up onto his legs.

"Mr Brue Dragon!" Mei shouted frantically at the huge animal. "Prease call White Crane for White Tiger. Led Phoenix love Brue Dragon if do this. Prease, Mr Brue Dragon!"

"Will she? Really love me?"

"Yes, Mr Brue Dragon!"

The dragon then opened his huge mouth and emitted an extraordinary and deafening sound. The children had to cover their ears. It was a bit like the howl of a wolf, only a hundred times louder. The effect was amazing. Within seconds, White Crane was there at the cave entrance.

"Quick!" White Crane called to the children. "On my back immediately! Before Blue Dragon takes to the sky."

White Tiger and Mei splashed through the water and jumped onto the crane's back. Behind them a great deal of kerfuffle was going on as the dragon prepared himself for take-off.

"Hopeless flyer, he is," said White Crane as he lifted himself up into air. "Means well, but forever crashing into things. Could easily knock us out of the sky with that clumsy great body of his."

By now the Blue Dragon was jumping around outside on the ledge in front of the cave. Little fluffy clouds were coming out of his nostrils.

"Love-puffs, they are!" said White Crane when he saw the children looking at these.

Mei thought this was very funny, and started giggling away as she held on tightly to White Tiger.

"Zai jian!" the children shouted down to the Blue Dragon, but he was far too love-sick to notice them now.

"Just in time," said White Crane, as they soared into the sky. "He's got it bad, you know!"

White Tiger stared down at the Blue Dragon as the latter leapt into the air. He turned and spoke to Mei.

"How can he fly without wings?" he asked her, puzzled to see the Blue Dragon suddenly go shooting off in the opposite direction to them.

"Chinese dragon no need wings," the girl replied. "Fry by magic!"

White Tiger laughed.

"Fly, Mei, fly. Not fry!"

"Solly," said Mei, giggling. "Fly not fry. By magic!"

"Wow!" exclaimed White Tiger, as he watched the Blue Dragon darting this way and that in the sky before disappearing into a cloud.

"So, where to this time?" White Crane asked.

"Er…" White Tiger was a bit hesitant. "Could you…um…take us to the moon? Please?"

He expected an angry reply like 'don't be so stupid!'

"No problem," White Crane answered. "No problem at all. In fact, I wondered when you'd get round to paying Moon Rabbit a visit."

"You know him, then?"

"Of course I know him! We're the best of friends, me and Moon Rabbit."

"Oh!"

Almost nothing surprised White Tiger now. He had abolished all thoughts about gravity and space-suits and the like, and just clutched on tightly to White Crane. The sky was clear and the moon up there seemed to get larger and larger before his very eyes. They shot up and up into the darkening sky. Even the speed of the Qilin was nothing as compared with the rate at which they now travelled. Soon the moon was a vast white disc in front of them and the earth a beautiful luminous blue and white disc thousands of *li* behind them. The moon got larger, and the earth got smaller until they seemed the other way round. The moon was larger than the earth; an enormous cratered world ahead of them. Craters and mountains! That's all there seemed to be up there, and a very long way from Peebles.

However, just when White Tiger was beginning to feel very sceptical about the existence of a rabbit on the moon he spied something different to the side of a large crater. It was well-camouflaged since it was the same colour as moon rock, and White Tiger could quite see how it might have been missed by people looking at the moon through giant telescopes. It was a building. As they got closer he saw that it was not just any old building. It was a vast and beautiful palace, with elegant towers and turrets, spiral stairways and crescent moon bridges.

The moon palace, built entirely from precious blue-white moon crystal!

CHAPTER 7: MOON RABBIT

"Enjoy the ride, kids?" asked White Crane, after landing in a huge open square just in front of the moon palace. There was a single large tree in the centre of the square, and White Tiger couldn't help staring at a big, strong-looking man who was chopping away at the tree. He certainly didn't look like a rabbit.

"Great trip, but who's he?" White Tiger asked.

"Oh, him? Don't ask! He's been chopping away at that tree for as long as I can remember – and that's a few thousand years! Greedy guy, he was, you know. Whatever he asked for the Jade Emperor gave him down there. But on earth he was never happy. Always wanted more. Know the type? Then one day he said he wanted the moon, so the Jade Emperor sent him up here, having got really fed up with him by then. As soon as he got here he wanted to get back down to earth. The Jade Emperor said he'll send the man back if he can chop down that Cassia tree. Takes him all day. He falls asleep exhausted in the evening, and overnight he finds that the tree has grown back up, as tall as ever. So he's still here, chopping away."

"Sad story," said Mei.

She wanted to go over to the man to cheer him up, but White Crane managed to dissuade her.

"Afraid it wouldn't do any good, and we can't go against the Jade Emperor. It's that fellow's problem, anyway. Should have been thankful for what he had in the first place. Now…Moon Rabbit this way, please."

The children followed White Crane over a little bridge that led to a tall, blue-white crystal archway. They passed through this and on to the entrance to the moon palace. White Tiger still found it very hard to believe they really were on the moon, and without any breathing apparatus or space-suits. Also, he had no idea how they would be able to get to Peebles from the moon. It seemed to White Tiger an awfully long way round. Mei was clearly beginning to feel a bit nervous, for she took hold of White Tiger's hand. This made White Tiger feel strong and sort of important, and helped him to forget his own anxieties.

"Good flight?" someone enquired.

The voice sounded too squeaky to be White Crane. Besides, the bird had already asked him virtually the same question. White Tiger looked at Mei. It certainly wasn't *her* voice, and she appeared equally puzzled. He looked at White Crane, and the crane pointed to the ground with his wing. White Tiger looked down and there, hopping about, was a small white rabbit with pink eyes. Is this it? he thought, a little disappointed, although he didn't say as much. He had expected a far larger rabbit. Something at least the size of himself, and more important-looking than the little bunny at his feet. Perhaps a rabbit wearing a smart white suit and black bow-tie and probably smoking a Cuban cigar. But this little rabbit looked as though it had just hopped out of an Edinburgh pet shop…only it spoke!

The rabbit repeated its question and White Tiger saw its tiny mouth move as it spoke.

"Er…fine, thank you very much," said White Tiger. "Very nice flight, thank you."

"Bit small, isn't he?" he whispered on the side to Mei.

"Shhh!"

Silently, they followed White Crane and the hopping Moon Rabbit into the moon palace. They walked along gleaming crystal corridors, across lovely courtyards with transparent sculpted figures of elegant women and, of course, rabbits. They crossed numerous, delicately-carved crystal bridges as they penetrated further and further into the moon palace. It was the most amazingly beautiful building White Tiger had ever seen. Soon they were passing palatial suites of grand rooms, full of furniture and fittings of the same luscious crystal. Through the doorway of one of these suites White Tiger spotted a lovely, but sad-looking, Chinese woman. She sat combing her long, silky, black hair and was staring at a picture that lay on the bed beside her. Moon Rabbit turned and saw the children looking at this woman.

"Chang'e," he squeaked. "She's the Moon Goddess. Been here nearly as long as I have. Floated up to the moon after swallowing an immortality pill. Has to stay here on her own now. Very sad about that, she is, because she misses her husband, the great archer Yi, terribly. Always staring at his picture, all day every day! Mind you, I wish I could have got the recipe for that immortality pill she took. I've been trying to make an immortality potion myself for thousands of years."

White Tiger, who thought the Moon Rabbit hardly needed an immortality potion if he had already been going for thousands of years, asked whether this was the same Archer Yi who had shot down the nine Jun birds and had made the Jade Emperor angry.

"The very same!" affirmed the Moon Rabbit. "Yi can come and visit her here at times, but *she* can't leave the moon, despite being a goddess.

"Poor Chang'e," said Mei. "Wish could help her!"

"Can't make everyone happy, Pretty Flower," Moon Rabbit said. "There are some people, you know, who perhaps really don't *want* to be happy."

Mei frowned disbelievingly, but said nothing. White Tiger again thought how the girl cheered people up. People like himself, *and* qilins, blue dragons and grey tortoises!

The little entourage entered a comfortable and homely-looking room. It had two beds in it, a table and several chairs all made from white crystal.

"Your apartment, children!" exclaimed the Moon Rabbit. "Like it?"

"It's…er…well, it's beautiful, Mr Moon Rabbit," White Tiger said. "But we really hadn't planned on staying." He looked at Mei. "You see, Mei needs to…"

"Oh, stay as long as you wish," Moon Rabbit interrupted. "A thousand years if you want to! It's so nice to have decent company for a change. Can't get any conversation from those other two. None at all!"

Mei obviously thought White Tiger was looking a bit cross again for she gave him one of her little pinches and he kept his mouth firmly shut.

"Moon Labbit so clever," Mei said. "Brue Dragon say Moon Labbit *velly* clever. Know everything."

"Sensible dragon, that. Very sensible!" said Moon Rabbit, jumping up onto an armchair, and beckoning to the children to sit down as well. "Did he *actually* say that, Pretty Flower?"

"*Dui!*" Mei replied.

"With or without?" continued Moon Rabbit.

The children, now seated at the crystal table, looked at each other.

"What?" asked White Tiger.

"What?" echoed Moon Rabbit, looking equally puzzled.

"With or without what?" White Tiger repeated with a faintly audible sigh.

"A dash, of course."

"A dash of what?"

White Tiger was already feeling rather exasperated with the Moon Rabbit.

"Your drinks," explained Moon Rabbit. "Do you want them with or without a dash? White Crane is waiting for your answer so he can go and get your drinks of moon juice and the moon cakes. Bound to be both thirsty and hungry after your flight. And you have to consider altitude up here too. Oh yes, always have to think about altitude on the moon. Mustn't get dehydrated, you know. So…with or without? A dash, that is."

White Tiger, irritated, was about to say something, but Mei got in just in time.

"*Dui, xie xie*, Mr Moon Labbit," she said, smiling at the Moon Rabbit. "Hua-Mei love moon cake too."

"That's more like it! White Crane won't be long."

White Crane went scuttling off down the corridor, and White Tiger leaned across to Mei and whispered in her ear:

"Yes *what*?" he asked. "A dash of *what*? You only said 'yes' and 'thank you'."

Mei shrugged her shoulders.

"Not know, but make Mr Moon Labbit happy," she said quietly. The girl then continued to address the Moon Rabbit:

"Brue Dragon say Moon Labbit has answer for everything."

"Does he now? Very sensible dragon that. Eminently sensible. Mmm! Now, where were we? Oh yes. Myself! I was about to tell you children a little bit about myself."

White Tiger hoped it wouldn't be a long 'little bit' like a Grey Tortoise story.

"Are you sitting comfortably?"

"Yes, yes!" muttered White Tiger through his teeth.

"Then I'll begin. Mind you it's a *sad* story! Is that okay with you?"

The children nodded. White Tiger was getting very used to sad stories. Mei whispered to White Tiger that she knew the story of the Moon Rabbit already. Her *Kung-Kung* had told it to her when she was little.

"Once, a very long time ago, I was just an ordinary rabbit. The same me, only a more *ordinary* me. Then three old men came along. They were very poor. They seemed to have nothing at all. They asked us animals for food. The others gave the men food, but I had nothing to give apart from myself. So I told them I would hop into a cooking pot and they could eat *me* for food. This went down well with the Jade Emperor. Self-sacrifice, or something, he called it. So, as a reward, he turned me into a jade rabbit and sent me up here to live in the moon palace."

Moon Rabbit saw White Tiger looking at him in a funny way.

"Special *soft* jade, so I can hop about," he added. "Just like the Jade Emperor himself!"

"Mr Moon Labbit kind as well as know everything!" said Mei.

"Yeah!" agreed the Moon Rabbit, nodding. "Pretty knowledgeable."

"And Brue Dragon, he say Moon Labbit only one who know how send children back to Peebles. Only Moon Labbit know this."

"Really?" enquired the Moon Rabbit. "Peebles, you say?"

"*Dui!*"

"Well, you could, you know, sort of try to, er…um…in a manner of speaking, just *go* back to Peebles? That would be the best way, for sure. But why Peebles? I've never met anyone wanting to go to Peebles before. And I've been here for thousands of years!"

"Parents in Peebles. Miss very much," said Mei, starting to cry. "Mei so sad now."

White Tiger put his arm across the girl's shoulders.

"There, there," he said, glaring at the Moon Rabbit. "We'll get back to Peebles, you and I. Please don't cry, Mei."

"Miss *Baba* and *Mama* so much," sobbed Mei.

Moon Rabbit was beginning to look rather uncomfortable.

"Peebles…Peebles…let me see. Is that a country? Of course *I* know the answer, but need to know that *you* do too."

"Aye," said White Tiger angrily. "It's a *very* important country. Everyone back on earth knows about Peebles."

"And you have an emperor there? Of course you do, of course!" the Moon Rabbit muttered.

"Oh," replied White Tiger, his arm still across Mei's shoulders. "We have more than an emperor...we have a provost! Wears a gold chain around his neck and attends functions."

"A provost indeed! Yes, I must tell the Jade Emperor all about provosts and functions. Remind me to do that. Now Peebles...er...?"

White Crane reappeared balancing a tray on his outstretched wings. On the tray were four tall crystal glasses brimming with a clear, colourless fluid that looked to White Tiger just like...well, water, actually. There was also a plate full of small round cakes. Mei's eyes lit up when she saw the cakes.

"Real moon cakes!" she exclaimed. "Mei love moon cakes. Have every year in China at Moon festival. Each autumn when full moon."

White Tiger was so pleased she had stopped crying. However, her tears had made him absolutely determined to get her back home. And soon! For the time being, though, he agreed that they needed some refreshments. The Moon Rabbit continued to squeak away in the background about Peebles and provosts and functions and things. He reached forward and took a glass of moon juice and a moon cake, which he handed to Mei, and then took a glass and a cake for himself.

"Just love moon juice," said the White Crane, putting the tray in front of the squeaking rabbit, and picking up a glass and a cake before sitting down. "Such amazing stuff. Gets you anywhere you want to go. Truly amazing! One glass of this, a quick whiz round the magical crater out there and 'hey presto'! I'm back in my nest in Hangzhou, nice and comfy like. Never could understand it, but it saves all the bother of a flight back to earth. Particularly with the time lag thing. Otherwise I'd be back a whole day later."

White Tiger almost choked on a mouthful of moon cake. He looked at Mei whose pretty face had simply lit up at White Crane's casual remark. She obviously had precisely the same thought as White Tiger. Now they had a way of getting back to Peebles! Moon Rabbit continued to take little nibbles of moon cake, mumbling about emperors and Peebles and gold chains, and puzzling over the children's return to Peebles.

"Where's this magical crater?" White Tiger asked White Crane.

"Oh, just along the corridor, first left, second right and up the stairs. Can't miss it. Brings you out right at the top of the magical crater," explained the bird, spraying crumbs from a beakful of moon cake.

Mei turned to the Moon Rabbit.

"Oh, *xie xie*, Mr Moon Labbit," she said. "Moon Labbit so kind tell White Tiger and Hua-Mei how get back Peebles!"

"Peebles?" squeaked the rabbit.

"*Dui*! White Tiger clever, but still think not so clever as Moon Labbit. Now because of clever labbit can go home see *Mama* and *Baba* again!"

White Tiger and Mei winked at each other.

"Clever? Do you *really* think so?" asked the Moon Rabbit.

"*Dui*!"

"Well, I do think a lot. Perhaps *that* makes me clever. Was just thinking about that country called…er…um…Pobbles or something."

"Peebles," corrected White Tiger. "You've just shown Hua-Mei and myself how to get back to Peebles. Thanks, Mr Moon Rabbit!"

"Did I do that?" squeaked the rabbit. "Wow, I must be clever. Tell you the truth, I'm not even sure where Peebles is, you know!"

"You're not alone there, Mr Moon Rabbit," said the boy.

White Tiger remembered going on a school trip to Belgium the previous year. There were children from other parts of Scotland and from England there, and *they* had no idea where Peebles was either.

"Well," said White Crane, standing up again after gulping down his moon juice. "Must be going now. Thanks for the moon juice, friend Moon Rabbit. Love the stuff. And you, Pretty Flower and White Tiger, hope to see you again soon. Perhaps in that funny country of yours. Pebbles, or something?"

"Peebles!" laughed White Tiger.

"Anyway, you're in good hands here with my friend, Moon Rabbit. Helpful sort of chap, he is! *Zai jian!*"

"*Zai jian*, Mr Crane!" the children called out in unison.

"*Xie xie*," added Mei. "Mr Crane so kind. Velly kind!"

In an instant White Crane was gone. White Tiger knew he should have felt frightened up there on the moon, so far from home and with their only obvious means of transport back to earth having just rushed off, but he wasn't the slightest bit scared. Not even when the Moon Rabbit began squeaking to himself again about blue dragons and the Monkey King and provosts from Peebles. Perhaps being there with Mei helped him to overcome his fear.

Mei spoke to the Moon Rabbit:

"Mr Moon Labbit. When get to magical crater, which way go?

"You? Magical crater? Why?" asked Moon Rabbit.

"Clever Mr Moon Labbit say this how get back to Peebles, Hua-Mei and White Tiger."

"Did I?" enquired the Moon Rabbit. "Did I say that? How clever of me! Well, ever looked at a drop of water in a full bath when you take the plug out?"

White Tiger couldn't see what that had to do with getting back to Peebles. Besides, how could you look at just one drop in a bath full of water? Nevertheless he remained patient. Mei had already taught him the importance of patience.

"No," he replied morosely.

"Well," continued Moon Rabbit, "that drop of water will want to get back to the sea since that's where all water comes from on earth. Like you children come from Peebles, eh?"

"Aye," said White Tiger grumpily.

"So, how does that drop get from the bath water to the sea when you take the plug out?" asked Moon Rabbit.

"Well, it goes down the flipping plug hole, of course!"

White Tiger began to feel himself getting rather cross again, what with all this useless talk about baths and plug holes.

"Yes, but which way, White Tiger? Which way round does it go?"

The boy was just about to blurt out something very rude when a soft little pinch from Mei stopped him. She put up her hand.

"Prease, Mr Moon Labbit," she said. "Like *Zhong*? Water drop go round like crock hand get to sea."

"Top of the class, Pretty Flower! Clockwise! That's how you and White Tiger must run from the top to the bottom of the crater. As fast as you can. If you *really* want to get back to where you come from, that's how you do it. Like that drop of water wanting to get back to the sea, you'll get back to Peebles."

White Tiger and Mei grinned at each other. At last, thought White Tiger, we're getting somewhere! Moon Rabbit suddenly frowned. He looked very pensive.

"Pretty Flower also comes from Hangzhou. Right?"

"*Dui!*" the girl replied.

White Tiger was getting the drift, and he didn't relish the thought of Mei ending up in China again, and with him safely back in Peebles.

"White Tiger, you must hold on to Pretty Flower's hand all the time. Don't let go for a second or she could end up in Hangzhou. I wouldn't like that and neither would the Jade Emperor."

White Tiger looked at Mei. He would hold her hand as tightly as she would let him when the time came. Perhaps Moon Rabbit was wiser than he had thought.

"So, holding hands you run clockwise round the magical crater," continued Moon Rabbit. "You'll have to run faster and faster and faster, just like that drop of water, until WHOOSH! Down through the plug hole you go. You know, right now I expect White Crane is safely tucked up in his nest in Hangzhou."

Even after hearing all this White Tiger wasn't scared. They hadn't taken their moon juice yet, and he looked at the tall crystal glass full of clear fluid on the table before him. He glanced at Mei. She smiled and nodded, and he nodded back. They raised their glasses together and began drinking the moon juice.

White Tiger was so surprised. He could never have imagined how good that clear, colourless fluid would have tasted. It was like a blend of all the fruits he had ever eaten, and yet there was still more. Other flavours so delicious that he wanted the drink to go on for ever. These flavours also seemed to bring back memories. Memories of his home and parents and friends in Peebles. In his mind he could see the River Tweed and the hills around Peebles. He even saw a No. 62 bus go by. In his mind, that is. When he had finished the drink he put down the glass and looked at Mei. He noticed a troubled look on her face, and realised she must have had conflicting images in her own mind. Her parents in Peebles and her new friends Amy and Andy, but maybe she had also seen her *Kung-Kung* and her friends in Hangzhou. White Tiger took hold of the girl's hand, and she smiled at him. He vowed not to let go of her hand until they were back in Peebles.

"Well, Mr Moon Rabbit," said White Tiger, "it really has been nice knowing you. I'm sorry we have to leave already."

"*Dui,*" added Mei. "Go back Peebles, see *Mama* and *Baba* again."

"So soon?" queried Moon Rabbit. "Oh dear! I had hoped for a little more company. Maybe just a few hundred years, eh? Would that make so much difference back in Peebles?"

"You have Chang'e, and the guy chopping away at that tree outside," said White Tiger.

"Oh, they're no company at all."

White Tiger held Mei's hand firmly when she stood up and gave the rabbit a kiss on the forehead.

"Lovely Mr Moon Labbit, but must go now." she said.

White Tiger thought the Moon Rabbit had turned a slight shade of pink.

"White Tiger and Hua-Mei say to people and labbits in Peebles how kind is clever Moon Labbit. Also velly wise."

"Well, just here to please," said the Moon Rabbit, looking embarrassed. "You know, I hadn't been kissed for thousands and thousands of years, Pretty Flower. Could you...you know...just another little one? A wee one?"

Mei gave him another little kiss and stroked his ears. The rabbit most definitely went pink after that.

"Remember what White Crane told you," he said to the children. "First left, second right and up the stairs. And hold on to Pretty Flower, White Tiger. Look forward to meeting up again. Particularly you, White Tiger, since you're the guardian of both the moon and of white jade. Pay me another visit, please do. Perhaps in the year of the rabbit, eh? We can have another chat about provosts and functions and dragons."

White Tiger didn't have the heart to tell Moon Rabbit that the White Tiger who was guardian of the moon and of white jade was surely a different White Tiger from himself. After all, he was really only Stevie Scott from Peebles. Nevertheless, he wished to remain his *own* White Tiger in the company of Pretty Flower.

"You, White Tiger and Pretty Flower, together you're like Yin and Yang!" Moon Rabbit continued.

White Tiger looked at Mei. He thought Yin and Yang sounded like a pair of circus clowns, or something.

"Who are they?" he asked.

Mei smiled.

"Moon Labbit give big compliment. Yin and Yang in everything. Like balance. Always balance. Boy 'Yang', girl 'Yin'. Same as man and woman, day and night, light and dark, heaven and earth. *Kung-Kung* teach me. Need Yin and Yang together to get good balance. Then good thing happen. Mr Moon Labbit give *velly* big compliment."

Mei squeezed White Tiger's hand.

"You mean he thinks we get on well together?" asked White Tiger.

"More," said the girl quietly. She blushed and looked away.

So, after bidding the Moon Rabbit farewell, the children left hand-in-hand, taking first left and second right along the crystal corridor, and then up the staircase at the top of which they found themselves at the rim of a huge white crater. It was smooth and shiny, like a giant porcelain sink, and way down there, at the bottom, was a small black hole through which White Tiger knew he would have to fall whilst holding on to Mei. Still he had no fear. He just wanted to get Mei back to her parents in Peebles.

"Okay?" White Tiger asked his friend, gripping her hand.

"*Xing!*" she replied, smiling.

They perched themselves right at the very edge of the magical crater.

White Tiger counted:

"One, two, three…NOW!"

The children ran off to the left in a clockwise direction round the steeply sloping side of the crater. They had to run fast to stop themselves just slipping straight down towards the hole.

Faster and faster, until soon they were whizzing round the crater, and gradually White Tiger could feel himself being sucked towards the small black hole. Faster and faster they went, down and down into the crater and the hole below them got larger and larger. They were spinning in smaller and smaller circles until suddenly, whoosh…PLOP! They went through the black hole at the bottom of the magical crater.

CHAPTER 8: CHANGES AT THE ROMAN CAMP

"He's awake!" someone shouted.

Stevie Scott had just opened his eyes and was blinking. He felt very snug and saw that he was lying in a warm and comfortable bed with clean-smelling, smooth, white sheets as pure as the crystal moon palace! The person who had shouted was a young woman in nurse's uniform. How strange, Stevie thought. Somehow he had expected it to be a rabbit or a tortoise speaking – or even some sort of bird!

"And so is Maisie!" the nurse exclaimed excitedly, after turning to glance in the other direction. Stevie propped himself up on his elbows and looked at the bed opposite his. A Chinese girl with long black hair and a friendly smile was looking at him. She waved, and Stevie waved back at her.

"*Ni hao*, Mei!" he called out. "*Xing*?"

"Okay, White Tiger!" she called back.

"Hey, Mei, what's 'the year of the rabbit' mean?"

"Twelve animals each have special year. Call Chinese calendar. Labbit, dog, pig, sheep. Even tiger and dragon. Animal years always follow same way. Like this."

Mei traced a circle in the air with her hand.

"A cycle? Like days of the week?"

"*Dui!*" answered Mei. "Chinese new year January or February. Big festival in China for new animal year. People born same animal year have same…"

Mei paused and frowned. She was trying hard to think of the right English word. Stevie was very good at words.

"Characteristics?"

"Cha…lact…er…listics!" Mei giggled. "Think so!"

"Which animal are we, Mei?"

Stevie knew already that the girl's birthday was a week after his own in April.

"Year of ox," she replied. "Hua-Mei and White Tiger year of ox! Ox people make friends easy. Work hard. Always trust ox people!"

They both laughed when Stevie started to go 'moo, moo!'

Stevie flopped back onto his soft pillow feeling very happy, for it hadn't all been just a dream! I really *am* White Tiger, he thought. The nurse, who had rushed out of the room on seeing both the children awake, now returned with four adults: his Mum and Dad, Maisie's Mum, whom he recognised, and a Chinese man with a smile just like Mei's. Stevie's own Mum was in tears as she hugged the boy. After Mei's parents had been reunited with their daughter, Mr Wu came across to Stevie's bed.

"Hi! I'm Maisie's dad. Maisie told me it wasn't your fault at all, Stevie. Please don't feel bad," he said, shaking Stevie by the hand. "We're all just so relieved you're both better now. Your friend, Andy, and his brother, Ross, told us how you saved Maisie's life. They saw you dive in after her. We can't thank you enough, Stevie!"

Mrs Scott looked at her son very proudly.

"Perhaps you could give Maisie swimming lessons some time," she said, for she knew what a good swimmer he was. Stevie liked the idea of teaching the girl how to swim.

"You were both pretty poorly when Ross fished you out of the river, Stevie," his mother continued. "They called a 999 ambulance and rushed you into the Borders General Hospital. You were on breathing machines in Intensive Care. They brought you down here this morning and the sedative's only just worn off now. The doctors say you'll both be fine. Back to school in a few days, they say."

Stevie and Maisie had a lot to talk about over the following three days in hospital before getting home. Maisie (or Mei, as Stevie preferred to call her) was certain it was White Tiger's courage that had saved them in China, whilst Stevie (or White Tiger, as Mei liked to call him) insisted it was the girl's wisdom and charm that got them back home to Peebles. At the end of the day they decided it was all due to Yin and Yang!

"Mei?" White Tiger asked, on one occasion. "What I can't understand is how the Jade Emperor knew about us coming to get the red pearl and the magical staff back for the Blue Dragon. His messengers seemed to have told everyone about us in advance and even taught them to speak English. What if he had actually planned it all? Like arranged for your dad to get that job in Edinburgh so that we could meet up. Maybe he even got the mother duck to walk past our Roman camp each morning, just so that you might fall in the river?"

They both laughed.

"My *Kung-Kung*, he say our destiny," the girl replied.

"Would like to meet your granddad, Mei," White Tiger said. "Have you asked your mum yet about him coming to Peebles?"

"*Dui*," she replied happily. "Ask he come in time for moon festival. Bring moon cakes!"

"Great," said White Tiger. "Love moon cakes!"

Back at school all their schoolmates wanted to know exactly what had happened.

"Oh, just went to see the baby ducklings and fell in the water," said Stevie. "Woke up in hospital. That's all that happened, wasn't it, Maisie?"

"Yes," she said, winking at Stevie. "Baby ducklings. That's all!"

Stevie and Andy became the school heroes for rescuing Maisie, although both of them knew it was really Ross who had saved Stevie's and Maisie's lives. Mr McKinnon gave the whole school a talk about the danger of playing near the River Tweed.

"And always make sure there's an older person nearby, like Stevie and Andy did. You see how easy it could be to drown. If Andy's brother, Ross, hadn't been with them, Stevie and Maisie might not be with us today."

Stevie felt rather guilty about having hoped that Ross wouldn't appear and spoil their Roman breakfast that morning!

"Now, children, as Mrs Kerr promised you, we'll be watching Mulan this afternoon. All about a Chinese princess long ago. Before that, though, little Maisie has kindly agreed to tell the class a few things about her country. Some of you may have thought of some questions about China that you'd like to put to her."

At lunch break, Stevie, Andy, Maisie and Amy got together. Stevius Maximus and Andius Minimus informed the girls that they were invited to join the Roman legion. Maisie was to be a Romano-Chinese princess called Princess Hua-Mei, and Amy was to be her lady-in-waiting.

"What's that?" Amy asked.

Stevius Maximus wasn't really sure, but he was certain that queens and princesses *all* had ladies-in-waiting.

"They're very important," he replied. "And they're sort of waiting to be princesses too."

Amy seemed happy with that. She liked Maisie very much and was so pleased to be the Chinese girl's friend.

That afternoon Maisie stood beside Mrs Kerr in front of her class. First Mrs Kerr told them a few things about China and about the Chinese language.

"Do you know, children, Chinese is a very difficult language for us?" she said. "Not only is the writing difficult, because it uses lots and lots of symbols for syllables instead of our phonetic Roman lettering (Stevius Maximus and Andius Minimus exchanged knowing glances at the mention of the Romans), but the spoken language is tonal. That means it has ups and downs, like singing, and a word that sounds the same to us might mean something very different to the Chinese if you get the tone wrong. For example '*ma*' means mother in Chinese, but '*ma*' with a different tone could also mean horse, and a different tone still and it means something rather rude."

Maisie proceeded to demonstrate the different tonal pronunciations for 'mother' and 'horse' in Chinese. Then Maisie talked about China. Her father had given her a large map of the country to show everyone, and Maisie proudly pointed out Hangzhou where she came from and where her *Kung-Kung* was. She showed them the Chinese capital, Beijing, and then the largest city in the world, Chongqing. Stevie put up his hand.

"Do you know where Tai Shan, the holy mountain, is, Mei…er…Maisie?" he asked.

Maisie smiled, and pointed at a spot on the map somewhere between Beijing and Hangzhou.

"Ah! *Xie xie...*I mean thank you," he said.

Maisie giggled. The others were most impressed by Stevie's knowledge about things.

"Who was your best friend in China, Maisie?"

It was Amy who asked this.

Stevie looked anxiously at Maisie, but she had no hesitation in answering Amy's question. None at all!

"Best friend White Tiger," she replied. "Velly kind, velly blave."

She then reached up and whispered something in Mrs Kerr's ear. Mrs Kerr smiled.

"Maisie says White Tiger is very handsome too!"

Stevie felt his face going extremely red. So red that he thought it might catch fire! Andy looked at him.

"Hard luck, Stevius Maximus," whispered Andy.

Stevie just stared at his hands.

"Can I be your best friend in Peebles?" Amy asked.

Maisie smiled.

"In Peebles many best friend. All so kind."

With that everyone clapped. Maisie had become so popular Crazy Davie, Muckle Mikey and Red-nosed Rosie would never have dared tease the girl now. In fact Rosie was quite upset to find that Maisie had been moved and was sitting next to Amy.

For the first several days after returning to school Stevie had difficulty concentrating on the lessons, for his mind would keep taking him back to that other place – ancient China. He wanted to learn so much more about the country, about modern China, and about the customs and ways of Chinese people. Mei had a lot to teach him, he thought, and he was really looking forward to seeing her *Kung-Kung* in the autumn. He had also come up with a plan. He would have to discuss it with Andius Minimus, for it affected the legion in a big way. Perhaps, he thought, he should also talk to Mr Gordon, the fellow in charge of the Trimontium Museum in Melrose, for *he* knew everything that there was to be known about the Romans.

Stevie's plan was this: they would become *Chinese* legionaries. Of course, he realised it wouldn't be that simple. First they would have to arrange a treaty between the Romans and the Chinese. Mr Gordon might be able to help them there. Then they could form an alliance. Stevie knew that allies fought together at times. An alliance would give them an excuse to turn the Peebles camp into an outpost of the newly-formed Scottish Borders Chinese Legion. It seemed a great idea, and it would be easier for him, as White Tiger, to protect their Chinese princess. They would have to come up with a Chinese name for Andius Minimus, of course, and for Mei's lady-in-waiting, Amy. But these were all difficulties that would be easily overcome. And then Princess Hua-Mei could dance for them when her legionaries returned to camp weary after battle. Yes, it all made sense, thought Stevie, as he struggled with complicated long division in class.

That day, after school, Andius Minimus accompanied Stevius Maximus and Princess Hua-Mei as far as the corner of his street. As yet, Andius Minimus was unaware of his co-legionary's plan.

"*Zai jian!*" Stevius Maximus said to his friend.

"What's that?" asked Andius Minimus, bemused. Maisie laughed.

"*Zai jian!*" repeated Stevius Maximus. "It means 'bye!' We're both gonna have to learn Chinese now, I'm afraid. I'll be seeing Mr Gordon at the weekend, but from now on our camp will have to be a Chinese camp. It'll be easier for Princess Hua-Mei and her lady-in-waiting, you see. Then they won't have to learn Latin. Of course we can continue to speak Latin sometimes because there'll still be Roman legionaries around, but we'll be their Chinese allies in our camp in Peebles, so we've *got* to learn Chinese."

Andius Minimus knew Amy was now a lady-in-waiting, and would in all probability become a princess too in the near future, so it seemed a pretty good idea to him.

When Andius Minimus had left them, White Tiger turned to Pretty Flower.

"You do have one of those dance dresses – the ones with the long sleeves – don't you?" he asked the girl. Pretty Flower laughed again.

"*Dui,*" she replied. "Different colours, different dances!"

"One for the Grey Tortoise dance?"

"*Dui!*"

"And…er…" White Tiger was turning slightly pink. "What about the…um…White Tiger dance?"

Pretty Flower smiled.

"Ask my *ma* to make one for White Tiger dance. *Velly* special one!"

"Your *ma* must be very clever," said White Tiger.

Pretty Flower giggled.

"Way you say '*ma*' funny. In Chinese mean 'horse'."

Pretty Flower proceeded to teach White Tiger how to say 'mother' instead of 'horse' in Chinese. He realised he would need to work hard at his 'tones' if he were ever to master the Chinese language!

They had agreed to meet up and go to the Roman camp after tea that evening, with absolute promises to Maisie's parents that she wouldn't go anywhere near the water. They had some important things to sort out together because, as Stevie told his own parents, it was a very Yin Yang business setting up a Chinese camp. Maisie would *have* to be there, he explained.

White Tiger took Pretty Flower back to the camp by the river. It was whilst they were clearing away some weeds and tall grass to make a Chinese dancing area that he noticed a yellowing sheet of paper lying under a stone. He picked it up. The paper looked very old, and the writing was all in Chinese.

"Wow!" he exclaimed. "Look at this, Mei. Can you read it? What does it say?"

Pretty Flower took the paper and stared at it, her mouth open in disbelief.

"Message from Jade Emperor," she said softly. "It say *xie xie* to White Tiger and Pretty Flower. Say..."

She looked up at White Tiger, and grinned.

"Say Brue Dragon and Led Phoenix get married and..."

She looked down at the paper again.

"Say Monkey King jump thousands of *li* from Lord Buddha hand and go on great journey to end of world where find five tall pillar. Then..."

Pretty Flower covered her mouth and laughed.

藍龍和紅鳳結婚

感謝白虎和花美

玉皇大帝

"Then monkey pee on pillar to prove escape from Buddha hand. When monkey find Buddha again tell him this and say 'now make me immortal!' But Lord Buddha just open hand and show Monkey King wet patch where monkey pee on his finger."

The children laughed.

"So the Monkey King still has lots to learn!" said White Tiger.

When they were finished he escorted Princess Hua-Mei back to her palace in Peebles.

Oliver Eade, the author, woke up very early one cold autumn morning with a story in his head. He wrote it down long-hand and went back to sleep. Since then he's never stopped writing. He is particularly fond of fantasy and the timelessness of mythology from different cultures across the globe, often reflected in his writing for younger people.

Having lived in London, Southampton and America, he and his Chinese wife now stay in the Scottish Borders. They travel regularly to China where Moon Rabbit was conceived in 2006.

Alma Dowle, the illustrator, studied at Newcastle College of Art and loves illustrating children's books. She lives in the Scottish Borders where she taught art in primary schools for many years. Her joy is to draw and paint and share her gift with others.

For more information about the author visit: www.olivereade.co.uk
Visit White Tiger and Princess Hua-Mei at: www.moon-rabbit.org.uk

Praise for Moon Rabbit:

'Moon Rabbit will lead children's imaginations to fantastical realms. It is a magical mix enhanced by gentle and ethereal illustrations.'
Mairi Hedderwick, author of the Katie Morag books

'A thrilling read, a real page turner.'
Jenni, 12 and Ellen, 11

'An adventure fantasy. Prepare for a roller coaster read.'
Inayat, 12

'An ingenious and original adventure story for children which also offers them an intriguing introduction to a culture that will loom ever larger in their future lives.'
Roger Silverman, teacher and journalist

'"Magical" is the word for Moon Rabbit because it entrances and enchants both in words and because of its beautiful illustrations.'
Elisabeth McNeill, author